# RIORDAN

## HARRISON AMBUSH BOOK 1

## KATHI S. BARTON

**World Castle Publishing, LLC**
Pensacola, Florida
Copyright © Kathi S. Barton 2015
Hardback ISBN: 9781629893525
Print ISBN: 9781629893532
eBook ISBN: 9781629893549
First Edition World Castle Publishing, LLC, October 19, 2015
http://www.worldcastlepublishing.com

Cover: Karen Fuller
Editor: Eric Johnston
Editor: Maxine Bringenberg

# CHAPTER 1

He'd wanted to get to his office and change into a clean shirt, but his mom had been waiting for him. And when she'd ordered—yes, she'd ordered—him to sit, he did. This day could not get any worse. He was sure now, however, that it was about to.

"Your dad told me that you got into a fight with the local baker. And when you tried to molest her, she fought back. Would you mind telling me why you thought it was a good idea in the first place to have a public and very…well, colorful, fight in my favorite place to get bread?"

"It's nothing. Just a misunderstanding on her part. Her temper was out of control for no reason and she started throwing a fit. I'll take care of it tomorrow. Can I go now?" She told him to sit again. "I needed something from her, and she got mad at me. It's nothing, I assure you."

"Yet here you sit covered in jelly and custard, and all you have to say for yourself is it wasn't your fault."

Riordan wanted to point out again that he hadn't done that much to her that warranted her having a temper tantrum, but his mom did not look like she was going to listen. It was women, he decided, that had the foul moods all the time. Men were not prone to acting like the world was coming to an—

"Riordan, if you don't answer me, I'm going to use my favorite rolling pin on your thick head, and then I'm going to be even madder at you. Because I'm sure rather than knocking sense into your head, all it's going to do is crack this wood."

"She's my mate." Her foot started tapping, and he tried to think. But his dad came in then and sat down and started laughing. "Ask him. He was right there when she got it into her head to start hurling Danishes at me."

"I was there, love. And she did. But I'm thinking it might have been due to what he said to her and the way that he was pressing her against the wall with his big body. That's not what she called him...let me see, what was it? Ah yes. I believe she called him a hulking monster that had no more brains than...well, love, you get the idea. I will say that her mouth and language are a little on the rough side, and she made her point quite...loudly. But she did toss him around like he was nothing more than the child he was acting like. I would have kicked his butt, too, but her friends, two elderly women who would have made me think...well, they had it under control, sadly." His mother huffed at him, and her foot took on a speed that had him thinking he was as good as dead. His dad cleared his throat, and he looked at him. "Son, you have a bit of jelly hanging off your ear that looks like one of them dangling earrings your mother likes to wear."

"She won't let me clean up." He knew that he'd spoken loudly when his dad cocked a brow at him. "I'm a grown man. Not some teenager that has gotten caught with a girl in the back seat."

"No, you're a grown man, or so you keep telling me, that has made your own mate so angry with you that she's thrown her hard-earned product at you and has threatened to have you arrested if you come near her again." Riordan looked at his mother as his dad continued. "And if you want us to treat you like you're all grown up, I would suggest that you begin to act like it. This is no behavior for a man who is in charge of a large corporation, as well as one that hits the papers more often than not because he's such a humanitarian and a calm and level-headed man. You were not very level-headed, nor calm, today. What do you think they'd put there now if they were to see you like this?"

He knew just what they'd say. He'd fallen off his rocker. But as his parents continued to talk, he thought about the woman. She'd been…she'd been perfect, except for her temper. And if she was going to be his mate, that thing was going to have to be simmered down a bit. There was no way he could have her flying off the handle like a harpy when she got her panties all in a bunch.

He'd only gone in with his dad because he'd heard him go on about the place. All he'd talked about for the last month was the way this bakery made cheese Danish, and how they were flaky enough to make you beg for more. He'd even gone on to say that he wanted to invest in the place. And that was another reason Riordan had gone with him. No one was going to take his family for a ride.

As far as space was concerned, the shop had it. The wraparound counter seemed to scream at you to come and look what delights were there. It was well lit, the glass sparkling clean, and the baskets were overflowing with an array of pastries and breads that made his mouth water. Even from the doorway he could smell the yeast and jellies, blackberry and strawberry. A coffee station sat on one side to the room with a carafe of water for tea, it said, and baskets of tea flavors that had him wanting to check them out.

The two women behind the counter seemed to be working to their own music. They moved and slid around each other as if they'd been doing it for years, and not just the month that the shop had been open. They laughed with their customers, handed out samples big enough to look like a serving, and gave small ones cookies hand over fist. Whoever their marketing manager was had it right. The only way to make money was to spend a little.

A woman had come from the back with a tray of the most beautiful loaves of bread he'd ever seen. Then he'd gotten her scent. And Christ, it had been all he could do not to—

"Riordan." Riordan looked at his mother. She had been talking to him, and he had missed it all. "I asked you three times now what are you going to do to repair this. Because you will, or so help me, I'll make you wish that you had."

"Repair what?" She bounced the rolling pin—her favorite—in her left hand like she was thinking it was his head. He had to think what he had to do to make her soften her glare. A glance at his dad was no help, as he was laughing again. "I don't know what I did wrong that you think I need to fix. You should talk to her about what she's going to do about telling me she's sorry."

Riordan thought he heard his dad say, *oh brother,* but he wasn't sure, because at that moment his mother slammed the pin down on the table so near to his arm he thought that she had cut that pretty close. But then…maybe she'd been trying to hit him. When she went to the door and opened it, he sat there, not sure what to do. It was Sunday after all.

"Get out." He looked at his dad, who was not only no longer laughing, but looked a little scared himself. "Get out of my house right now and don't return until…until…get out of here right now."

"Mom?" She pointed out, and he had no choice but to move out or something was going to befall him that was going to be talked about in this family for the next couple of generations, if not forever.

Riordan moved out the door and turned to ask her what he'd done. But the door slamming in his face made him feel stupid…and a little pissed off. He was thirty-five years old, not some kid.

As he made his way to the truck, his brother, Mac, pulled in the drive. Riordan didn't even bother stopping to warn him, but got in his own truck and left.

"They're all nuts." Riordan turned the radio up as loud as he could to drown out his thoughts, then turned it down. He was pissed, but blaring his music wasn't going to make it go away. Instead, he lightened his foot on the accelerator and tried not to drive angry. That was all he needed to do, have an accident that would make his mom really mad at him.

Riordan liked to think of himself as a cool and very rational man. He thought things through before speaking, his plans were flawless when he put them out for people to see, and he never did anything on the spur of the moment. He liked order, planning, and a calendar. Doing things off the cuff or sly, as his brother, Ennis, called it, was not his way of working, not in business or his personal life.

The calendar on his phone was as filled as the one on his secretary's. The ones on his computer in his office as well as his house were updated daily. And if there was something that had to be canceled or moved, he'd go over the entire month to make sure that it didn't conflict with something else. Riordan was a man who did not like surprises. And finding out that the woman in the shop was his mate had messed up his entire schedule for the day.

"What did she think she was doing throwing me out?" Riordan wasn't sure if he meant his mom or the woman, but they both had done it. "It's Sunday, after all, and we have dinner as a family. Was this worth Mom getting all upset and telling me to leave? No, it was not. This is her fault, too. The bakery woman's."

As he drove to his apartment downtown, he thought about the way she'd felt pressed against his body, and wondered not for the first time what she would feel like wrapped around him naked. He had to adjust his cock for the third time since getting in his truck.

She'd been coming from the back room, her arms loaded with loaves of bread, when she'd taken a short stumble. His only thought was to keep her from falling when he caught her scent. Then she'd told him to let her go, and he'd had to taste her. And just like that, her temper flared, and he could only stare at her. Who knew that being pissed off could be so sexy?

As he reached for her again, having put the bread on the counter, she'd backed up quickly. Putting up her hands to warn him off, he thought, did nothing to slake his need, and he backed her up more until she was pressed against the wall. Burying his nose into her neck had made him hard as stone, and he could think of nothing else but taking her to the floor and coming deep inside of her. Except that she'd unmanned him with her knee, and that had him dropping like a stone.

Then the projectiles had started flying. He'd been hit in the head with several of them before he could stand up. When he reached for her again, this time her hand was filled with more Danish, and he felt rather than saw her move. He was on his back and looking up at her before he could catch his breath. Then one of the older women was standing over him with a large knife in her hands.

"I think you have overstayed your welcome, young man." He nodded but was afraid to move. "You can crawl out on your belly or get up and walk out. Either way, she wants you gone. And I'm thinking that she might be right. I don't want to have to stab you to get you going. Unless you want me to."

"I need to talk to her." The woman told him he'd be better off talking to the door, which he'd better be going through rather than talking to her right now. "Can I at least have her name? I can call her later so she can tell me what she thought she was doing by this mess. Don't you think she overreacted, even just a little?"

"No, I don't think so." She pointed to the door again, and he got the idea that he was going to get nowhere with her. As he made his way to the door, his dad was paying for his purchases as if nothing at all had happened. He was going to have a talk to him as well. The man would surely have his side on this.

Only he hadn't. Not only had he laughed at him the entire way home, but he'd not agreed with him at all. Not about the woman being nuts, or about her blowing things out of proportion, nor did he think that she'd done a thing wrong. Riordan was going to go down there first thing Monday, which would mess up his entire morning, just so she could apologize to him. This was no way to start a relationship.

~~~

Storm washed down the wall where blueberry jam had stained it. She'd have to find the paint can in the basement to touch this up. The strawberry had washed off a good deal easier, but it was fresher. She thought that she'd grabbed that tray last when he'd—

"You scrub much harder and the wall will fall over. You thinking about that man?" Storm nodded at her aunt. "Yeah, he was a big guy. Pushy as hell, but a big one all the same. Can't seem to understand why you're all pissy with him. You're hurting now, aren't you, child?"

"Just a little, nothing I can't handle. He mentioned that I was his mate." She looked at Aunt Lynn when she huffed. Storm wasn't sure if it was because she knew she was lying about the pain or about the man. Either way, it was a moot point. "I don't have…he can't be my mate. I don't want him. And he won't want me once he sees what is under my clothing."

"No one is more concerned with that than you are." Storm knew that her aunt had never seen her body since she'd come home, so said nothing. "You still seeing that doctor? The one that says you need to have those drugs to help you sleep? You gotta see someone about that pain, too. We both know you're hurting."

"You know that I'm not seeing him." Aunt Lynn nodded. "I know that the VA pays for it, but it's stupid to take them when all they do is make me weirded out. I was sleeping no better with them than I was without. But I do go and talk to that lady shrink. She's not too bad."

The doc had been all right until about a week ago, right after Storm had told her that she wasn't going to be able to see her again due to her having a job now. It was as if she'd taken it personally. Storm knew that she had to see someone or be back in the hospital again, but she was trying to stand on her own two feet instead of depending so much on her family. It wasn't like she had to work for the money, but she needed to work to keep her body from tightening up.

"That man, do you suppose he'll come back here?" Storm didn't turn around as she spoke to look at her aunt, but heard her huff again. "The man that he came here with is a nice man. I like him. But as far as I'm concerned, I really could care less if that fucking bastard darkened my doorstep again."

"Sally and I will keep him in line now that we know about him. I'm thinking he will be back. He didn't strike me as a man that would give up too easily."

Storm had thought the same thing. But before either of them could say anything else, the bell over the front door sounded and Aunt Lynn went to answer it.

Storm Browning was a woman that few people knew well. She preferred it that way, more now than before she'd joined the army. She supposed her upbringing had had a lot to do with that...at least the first ten years of her life. Now her memories were nearly too much for her to deal with, and she had a shitload of them. Few of them nice ones.

Her men, nine of them when she'd gone in country— overseas—had been her friends, but they were all dead now. All but her. As she made her way to the oven again when the timer went off, she tried her best not to think of that day and what had happened. Instead, she thought about how many cookies she had left to bake.

The board that Aunt Lynn had put up for her was filled. It felt good to see so many orders there, but it made her a little nervous too. If she was in too much pain, she knew that either of her aunts could bake for her, but she wanted to keep them from having to lift so much. They were in their late seventies, both of them, and they were actually her great aunts. All the family that she had in the world.

The cookies were put onto the cooling rack, then she put more on the parchment paper to bake as the first batch cooled. She had a system. It wasn't a great one, but it worked for her.

Stretching her arm above her head to hear it pop, she had to hold onto the table when the pain took her breath away. Storm made her way to the cabinet where she kept her medications. It was time for the next round of drugs anyway, and she thought that having a pain pill was in order this time.

Moving slower now that it was getting later in the day, she sat down on the seat she used when she decorated if anything needed her attention. Since the man had left her, her back had been throbbing and her legs felt like rubber. Her body hurt now, and not just a little. There was more baking to do, and then there were the dishes to wash, but Storm wasn't sure she could do either without lying down for a bit.

Going to the front of the shop, she saw that her aunts were busy and went to talk to the man at the counter. He grinned at her when she welcomed him to The Bakery.

"Nice name. Simple and right to the point." Nodding, she waited for him to order or tell her what he wanted. He was dressed well, expensively, and he had a face that made her think she'd seen him before. "I need to get three loaves of rye and two of sourdough. And I'm supposed to ask you if there are any...let me see what Mom called them before I make a fool of myself."

She got his bread for him and put them into the long loaf bags she'd just gotten in. They were generic, but they served the purpose. He was still talking on his phone when the next man came to the counter. Storm wanted to ask him to wait for her aunts, but he looked like he needed more than what was on display.

"You Sergeant Major Browning?" Storm nodded, but looked around to see if anyone else had heard him. "I was told to come on down here and see if you could use some help. The lady at the VA, she said you were looking for someone to help wash up."

Taking him to the back room, she sat him on the chair she'd been in and asked him when he'd last eaten. He told her that it had been a couple of days, because the shelter wasn't open on the weekends. And he hadn't cared for the meal they had on Fridays either.

"It's Monday. What's your name, soldier, and don't lie to me again."

He straightened up in the chair and nodded to her. "I'm PFC Daniel Gunning, but I go by Danny. I don't have no problems with drugs or nothing. Just nightmares and so on. I get to where I can't leave my place. And when that happens, I lose my place in line at the food pantry. It's been a couple of days since I've...leaving the apartment kind of gives me the willies." She knew that feeling. "I heard from Nurse Mason that you were looking to find someone to come in some days and help out by washing up. You mean dishes, I'm suspecting."

"Yes." He looked around the room, then stood up...much easier than she could have today. She sort of envied his ease. "You can start today, but I'm feeding you first. And if you object then you can think of it as an order."

He nodded and moved to the table in the back of the kitchen. Storm went to the front to get a loaf of bread, and the man from earlier was still standing there. When she told him she was sorry, he winked at her.

"I saw you were busy. You going to hire him, Sarge?" Nodding, she told him not to call her that. "All right. But what were you, if you don't mind my asking? Air force? Army?"

"Special Forces. Did you ever find out what your mom wanted?" He told her that he needed a dozen filled donuts, he didn't care what flavors. As she filled his order, all she could think about was the man in the back.

He'd be a great help should he be able to show up to work daily. She knew how hard it was for her just to get out of the bed some days, the pain was so bad. When she had the thirteen donuts for the man, she let Lynn ring him out. But he stopped her before she could go to the back again.

"Are you sure it's a good idea for you to hire him? You don't seem to know anything about him other than someone sent him to you." She pulled away from his touch on her arm. "I'm sorry. I just—"

"I can take care of myself. I have been for a very long time. While I appreciate your concern, trust me when I tell you that he should be more afraid of me than I am of him." He nodded and then looked over her shoulder. She didn't have to look to know who stood there. He might have just been hired, but Danny was a soldier first and foremost. "Now, if you don't mind, I've had a bang-up day so far, and I'd really like to be left to my own council."

"I'm sorry." Storm nodded and moved to the back room. The man left a few minutes later, and Storm made Danny a sandwich. She also cautioned him about helping her out when he thought she was in trouble.

"I'm hurting, like you, but I can handle myself. There is no reason for us both to get into trouble with some over protective shit that thinks because I don't have a dick between my legs that I'm one of them fainting hearts." Danny grinned at her. "Next time, you just let me handle it. But if someone fucks with my aunts, you have my full permission to kick some ass, all right? And don't call me by my rank here. It's Storm, or Stormy if you wish. I left that all behind a while back."

"Yes, sir." He bit into his sandwich and finished chewing before he spoke again. "You're that CO that got all those guys out, aren't you? I heard about it when it happened. I'm really sorry."

"I don't talk about it. And if you want to continue working here, you won't either." He nodded again. "I'm not trying to be a bitch—well, I am, but I don't want to think about it anymore. The nightmares plague me as well."

"Yes, sir, I'm betting that they do. If you, you know, need to talk, I can listen to you. Won't say a word, just be here for you." He took another healthy bite, then continued. "I might need you, too. I won't mean to, but I might just need to...I get them willies I was telling you about, and you might have to talk to me. About nothing if you want, but I get myself scared to death sometimes. I won't hurt you, but I do get scared."

"I'm here." He nodded, and she walked to the board. She had no idea what it said at that moment; her eyes were filled with tears. Storm wasn't the whiney kind of woman. She wasn't even one to lean on people, even if she was falling over on her face with the need to. But there were times that hot tears could make her feel more alive than anything.

After a bit, she heard the water at the sinks turn on and Danny start to hum to the music that was playing in the front of the shop...soft country music that her aunts both loved to hear, and sometimes even sang to. Storm pulled the first of the orders down just as Aunt Lynn came into the back room. She had the nightly list of things that they were running low on up front.

"We're taking what is left to the shelter." Nodding, Storm made a mental note to save some food for Danny to take home with him when he left. But her aunt handed her a sack that she could smell the bread in. "How's your back, sweetie? Want me to stay and help?"

"I'm going to go up in a bit and take a little nap." Storm was pretty sure her aunt knew it was a lie. "Then I'll work on some of this and the front stuff."

"Don't work too much, honey. We'll make do with what we have, and tomorrow is a half day too, so we might be able to make it." Storm nodded and locked up after her aunts left. Going to the back room, she started measuring things into the big mixer. It was going to be a very long night.

# CHAPTER 2

Ordan Harrison waited in line to get his morning Danish. When he'd told his lovely wife, Bri, that he was going to check in on the girl, she'd told him that Mac had been in to see her last night. He'd known that she'd done it…the bread and dessert that they'd had last night could have only come from here.

"I had to know that she was all right. He's a big brute of a man to be tossing her around." Ordan asked her if she meant the girl or Riordan. Her grin had him laughing. "I would have loved to have seen that. Her throwing him over her shoulder like he was nothing more than a bothersome flea. And to have her tossing food at him? Why, it was everything I could do not to laugh right in his face when he sat there all covered in it."

"He was a sight. I laughed so hard on the way home that I near hurt myself. But I'm going to go by and see her anyway. Might even tell her how sorry I am that we raised him up to be such a fool." And now here he was, next in line, and he'd yet to see her. The woman at the counter winked at him when he told her what he wanted in the way of food this morning.

Sometimes it embarrassed him to no end when a woman flirted with him. Ordan had aged well, he knew, and he'd taken care of himself, but he still was never quite used to woman doing things like this to him. But he gathered his tongue up and told the woman what he was there for.

"Last I seen her she was in the back decorating some cookies for a party." He nodded and said he'd come back then. "You can go on back and talk to her. Don't be put off if she's a might short with you. She's not had the best of mornings, and I don't think she's been sleeping too well lately."

Ordan was assured that it would be fine, and he'd had the choice taken out of his hands when Lynn—according to her name tag—asked if he'd be so kind as to ask the girl if she had any more chocolate chip cookies hiding back there. Ordan moved through the opening into a land as foreign to him as another country. As far as he was concerned, the kitchen was a place to have a meal and to talk to someone if the boys were in there. But he had no more idea of how to cook an egg than most people knew how to overhaul an engine. Which he had no idea of how to do either. He was what his boys called mechanically miss-inclined.

She was sitting at a table with bags of colored things all around her, and it took him a moment to realize it was frosting. He itched to pick one of them up and squirt some onto his finger to see if it tasted as good as it looked on the cookie she had in her hand. When he moved to stand beside her, Ordan touched her gently on the arm to warn her that he was there. He didn't want to startle her too much.

Ordan had never seen someone react so quickly in his life, but he lay as still as he could as she held the gun to his forehead. He had no idea how he'd gotten down on the floor, nor how she'd managed to land atop him like she was, but he wasn't stupid enough to ask her that right then. Her hand not holding the gun was at his throat, and her legs were gripping his ribs tight enough to hurt. His cat was screaming to be let loose.

"Don't move." He didn't even look at the woman who spoke from behind him. "She don't know it's you just yet. Or even where she is. Just lay there and I'll talk to her."

Ordan thought that was a wonderful idea. Then Bri touched his mind. She must have felt his fear and was making sure he'd not hurt himself or no one else had hurt him. He wasn't sure he could have calmed her and his cat, too, so he asked her, very politely, if she'd let him get over this first.

*I will not. Tell me what is going on right this minute, Riordan Harrison, or so help me I'm coming there and tearing up some behinds.* He told her where he was and what he was currently doing. *She's going to kill you? Over what our son did to her? That's not right, Ordan; you have to tell her we tried.*

*I don't think she knows what she's doing. The woman with her, an aunt I think, is talking to her. But I can see her face, Bri, and she's not here. There is...fear. She's terrified out of her mind right now.* She asked him if he was in any danger from her. *No. I don't know why I know that, but if she had wanted me dead, I'd be dead.*

*That's not very soothing, love. Just...don't hurt her. And don't let her hurt you. Riordan would never forgive her.* He told her it might be a good thing if they didn't mention this to him. *Yes, I can see that you're right. Just...will you call me when she's better? I worry about you both now.*

Ordan listened to what was being said by the older woman. "You're not Sergeant Major Storm Browning anymore, darling. You're home. Listen to me, Stormy, and come on back. Sergeant Major Browning isn't going to hurt this man because you're home and safe. Do you know where you are?"

Ordan saw the moment when the girl realized what she was doing. She didn't move off him right away, but she did ask him if he was all right. He nodded slowly before answering her.

"The gun is biting into my head. Do you think you could ease up on it a bit?" She didn't move, and he started to ask her again when a tear rolled down her face and hit him on the cheek.

"I can't move." He nodded again and waited for her to explain, her voice only a whisper of a sound. "I'm hurting so bad right now that if I try to move, I'm going to scream. I'm very sorry that I'm hurting you, but my back is twisted up and I can't make any other part of me work right this minute. If it's any comfort to you, I've moved my finger off the trigger a little."

No, that didn't ease him in any way, but he nodded to her. Ordan lay as still as he could for as long as he could until he felt a shadow fall over him. The woman moved, then cried out, and Ordan wanted to tell her it was all right when the man spoke.

"Sir, I can lift you up if that'll help." The woman moaned at the man speaking. Ordan didn't take his eyes off the girl. Not because he was afraid she'd hurt him, but because he was afraid that she'd hurt herself more. "I can pick you up like those men did me when I first come out of my coma. I can do it if you let me." He actually put his hands on her shoulders.

"Don't touch me." He knew that it had cost her to scream at the man. He could see it all over her face. "I'm going to move my hand, and when I do, I'm going to see if I can roll to my back, all right?"

"Just stay still until this passes." Her laughter had him thinking she was rusty at this, at having any humor in her life. "I'm not going anywhere, and my wife is aware of what is going on. Do you know what I am?"

"Cat. Tiger." He nodded, impressed that she'd known. "You're the father of the idiot from yesterday. And if I'm not mistaken, related to the man who came in last night wanting to help me."

"Another of my sons, Mac. My wife sent him in. I have six sons, and only one of them is an idiot, as you've figured out. I'm not sure that the others won't be too when their time comes to meet their mates. Women can make us men do the dumbest things when our cat finds you." The gun moved, and he could feel it bite deeper into his skin, then the trickle of blood as it moved on his forehead. "Don't think about that right now. Just keep talking to me, all right?"

"I hurt." He knew that she did, and his heart twisted in pain for her. "I'm really sorry. I've been...I have a few demons that I'm working on."

"You're doing fine. Just fine." When the gun moved again, it was moved off him, not deeper into his flesh. "Your breads were a hit at dinner the other night. Too bad that Riordan wasn't there to enjoy them. His momma sent him home without his supper. She was in a fine spirit when she heard what he did to you. We were just laughing at how you'd sweetened him up with all those pretty things." He wasn't really babbling, he told himself, just trying to talk her down. Ordan thought it was calming him as well as his cat, but he kept an eye on her, too.

"I'm going to move now. Don't try to help me." Ordan nodded and felt her shift slightly above him. The gun was still there, he could feel it on his shoulder, but it wasn't pointed at him any longer, just there in her hand. When she closed her eyes, he could feel her tense up and wondered if she'd be able to make it. Then he was suddenly free.

The scream made him think they were under attack. He leapt up quickly to defend her when he realized nothing he could do would help the child. Her body was curled into a tight ball; her screams were bouncing off the walls until she just suddenly stiffened and lay still. It was then that he noticed that one of the older women who had worked the counter was shoving a needle into her bottom.

Checking for her pulse when she stopped screaming, he found it to be beating faster than that of someone running a marathon, and she was clammy to the touch. He wondered what was in the syringe.

"Pain killer, triple dose. I hated to do that to her, but she won't take it unless we make her. She's going to be mightily pissed off when she wakes up." As the medical kit was packed up, the woman continued talking. "I'm Lynn Payne. This is my sister, Sally Eaton. Stormy is our niece. In the event you didn't notice, she's been hurt something awful, and I don't just mean her body, either."

"You called her Sergeant Major Browning. Is she a vet?" Lynn said that she was. "I take it she's been hurt while in the line of duty. And recently, too, I'm thinking."

"Tore her up. They thought for sure she was dead when they pulled her out of that tree days after her Humvee was blown up." The man who had offered to pick her up handed him a cup of tea. "PFC Gunning, sir. But you can call me Danny. I heard all about her last tour. She's a hero to most of those boys she helped out before she was bombed."

"She's not going to thank you for telling on her, Danny. You go on back to those pots and I'll make you a sandwich here in a bit. " He nodded at the other woman as he moved away. Sally smiled at him. "I'm very sorry about this. She's going to be very embarrassed when she wakes, and will want to make it up to you."

"You said she was hurt. Badly. Is she going to be all right?" Neither woman said a word, nor would they look at him. "Did my son hurt her yesterday when he took advantage of her?"

"Yes."

Lynn said she was going to lock up now as it was after one. He'd forgotten that they closed early on Tuesday, and started to gather his things. His shoe had been knocked off him and had landed across the room. And he'd not gotten his Danish.

"You won't say anything to him, will you? She's going to be upset enough that she's done this to you." He started to ask Sally why she'd be upset when she continued. "You have to realize that she's not over this. Not any of it. For over two months they told her she'd never work again. Had specialists come in and talk to her about a different lifestyle that she'd have to adapt to. There would be no more walking without a limp they told her a few weeks after she proved them wrong about her getting around. She'd have to have a walker if she was up and about for more than a few minutes, they told her, and damned if my girl didn't make them shove that up their collective bottoms, too. But her body will betray her in the most difficult times now. The only thing they got even half right was that she'd be hurting...not just her body, but her mind, too. She still sees something that haunts her nightly. Or maybe it's something else that comes to her at odd times."

"When?" She looked away when he asked, so he asked her again. "How long ago did this happen to her? I'm thinking not long at all. She's hurting badly for someone that might have been out for a long time, I think."

"Fourteen months ago." He nodded and helped her pack up the things on the table. The poor girl just lay there on the floor until he asked if they needed help getting her to bed. "We can manage, Mr. Harrison. We've been caring for her since she's been home. And the longer that she lies there, the more the drugs will work throughout her system. She's going to cry again when we get her up from there. But she'll rest easy tonight. Not well, but easy."

In the end, he took her up the flight of stairs for them. She wasn't very heavy, and the staircase was wide enough that he could hold her without crushing her to his body. But Ordan knew that she was hurting no matter how gentle he tried to be with her.

As he lay her on the tiny bed, a cot really, Ordan looked around. No pictures adorned the walls, and he didn't see a television. The bathroom door was open, and he could see that her toiletries were laid out in a neat row, her towel folded beneath them. The kitchen had a single bowl in the drainer and no sign of a coffee pot or any other counter-top sort of things. He saw no canisters like his missus had, no plants in the window, and he couldn't see a single rug or other personal item anywhere. He didn't even have to ask to know that she'd more than likely been living here since she'd gotten released, and that she preferred it this way...no clutter in her life. Much like his own son did. Ordan had to smile to himself when he thought of the two of them together. It was going to be a sight to behold, he just knew it.

"I'll have to share with my wife what…she'll need to know because of her scent. But I won't tell anyone else what I've seen or heard." Sally told him thanks. "If she needs anything, and I do mean anything, give me a call."

He wrote down his home and cell phone numbers and gave them to the woman. But as he left, going to his car with a huge bag of breads and cakes, he knew they'd only call if it was an absolute emergency. And even then, it might not happen.

~~~

Riordan had a dozen red roses and a dozen yellow ones on the seat beside him. A tree in a balled bundle was in the back of his truck, as well as a flat of his mom's favorite flowers. He was going to grovel. He was willing to do most anything to get into his mom's good graces again. He had fucked up royally with her.

It had taken him the better part of the day on Sunday to realize that she wasn't going to call him and tell him to come for dinner. It was nearly seven o'clock when his belly told him that it was either go get something to eat soon or he was going to have to eat the left over left over's from last week's dinner for his own supper. He ordered a pizza and beer to have instead of the pot roast and new potatoes that he'd known they were having for dinner on Sunday.

On Monday he'd waited all day for his phone to ring to ask him to come home to make up. That was when he realized how badly he'd messed up with his mom.

When he'd gotten up yesterday morning, he called his office and found not only no messages from his mom, but his brothers hadn't called him either. Usually when he had to miss a dinner because of work, they would send him pictures of what he'd missed, as well as pictures of them all together having fun without him. There wasn't a single one this time.

He'd called the office just to see if there was an outage or something as he headed to the office yesterday. Now today, he was going to his mom's instead of to work where he should have been.

"Good morning, sir. I have some messages for you. I have cleared your morning for you as you asked me to last night. Also, your father said that he was going to come in and talk to you, and then a little bit ago, he called back to say that he'd changed his mind. He sounded upset. Is he all right?" Riordan assured her he was just fine. "I have three meetings for you first thing after lunch. Then there is the dinner thing you have with Miss Applegate."

He'd forgotten about that. Riordan would have to break that off with her. He had a mate now, and dating Isabell would be a waste of time. Things were going to have to change a lot now that someone else was going to be demanding some of his time.

"Call Miss Applegate and tell her that something has come up. And if you could, would you send her out a...no, make that two dozen roses. Sign it the usual way." She told him she'd do that now. "Also, could you do me a favor and look and see what you can find on a bakery called simply The Bakery? I've looked, but all I can find is that it's under new ownership. I had no idea there was even one there until Sunday."

"I can do that if you'd like. Would you like me to run the owner down as well? See what I can find there for you?" He told her that would be helpful. Riordan knew that she'd have everything there was to be had on this shop by the time he got to the office this afternoon. "Oh, sir, Mr. Mac was in this morning. He said he'd catch you later. I think he had something for you. I've cleared you an hour with him after lunch."

Mac wanted him? His brother was busier than he was most of the time, and was rarely in the offices. He was the hands on kind of guy, the one that got them the businesses and helped to calm nerves when it was evident that the business they were working for was going to have to be closed. As consultants, it was hard to tell someone that had been in business for more years than he'd been living that there was nothing they could do to help them.

Mac was his next younger brother by seventeen months. His real name was Cormac, named after their grandfather who had died just before Mac had been born. Mac was a great deal like the old man had been, or so their mother was fond of telling them. Where most people would find sadness in closing a business, Mac, like his grandda before him, would find the brightness in it. He was a forever optimist. Riordan liked to think of himself as a realist. It was what kept him grounded.

Aedan was born two years later and was an Irish twin to Darcy…meaning Aedan had been born January first the same year that Darcy had been born November thirtieth. And even though a few months separated them, they were as close as twins in nearly everything they did. For the company, the two of them ran point. Riordan had no idea why they called it that, but the two of them would go in first to a business that had called for help, work the lines or whatever was being done, and see if there was a way to help that way. Usually they could see a problem within days.

Liam worked in the office with Riordan. He would be the good guy to his bad. And lately it had seemed to Riordan that Liam was covering for him a great deal. Riordan's temper had been volatile to the point where he would skip meetings altogether rather than have everyone pissed at him for days on end. Liam was really good at calming the members of their staff.

Their baby brother, Ennis, had decided that he wasn't interested in becoming a part of Harrison Consulting. When he'd entered college, he decided that the firm would get along just fine without one more Harrison working for it, and so he had become a doctor. And from what he'd heard from Mom, he was a hell of a doctor, too.

Riordan's phone was ringing as soon as he pulled into his parents' driveway. He stopped the truck and turned it off before answering the call from Christina Smith, his secretary. She was talking with someone else when he answered, and he tried to hold his temper. It was one of his biggest pet peeves about people. If you call him then be ready to speak when he answered. Christina started talking just before he was ready to hang up.

"I've found out about The Bakery. I had no idea where you meant until I saw the article about it when I did a search. There's not much about the owners themselves, but I managed to find out a great deal about one of them. Her name is Storm Browning." The name meant nothing to him, and he told her that. "I'm sending you the link to your phone. You should read that before I go much further. I don't know why you want this information, sir, and I'm not one to pry. But if you plan to close this place down, I want you to know that I will quit right now."

"Why would you think I have intentions of closing the place down?" Then it occurred to him. "Mac told you what happened the other day, didn't he?"

"He did." While she was as professional as she always was, he could hear the anger in her voice. "And I, for one, would hope that you learn to curb your inner cat before you go in there again and have an entire platoon on your ass."

The phone didn't slam down, but it might as well have. He held onto his temper for as long as he could until he had to move. Leaving everything in the truck, including his phone, he got out and stretched. He needed a run and a hard one. Taking off his shirt and tie, he laid them neatly on the seat and then kicked off his shoes. As he made his way barefooted to the woods behind the house, he tried to think of where in the last several weeks he'd gotten so…so angry.

He knew that he'd been impatient at work, and short with a few people that he'd had to go back and apologize to. Then there were times when he'd snapped at his dad, his brothers...even his mom. And when he'd tried to think why, what had set him off, all he could think of was how pissed he'd been, but no reason for it.

His pants were off by the time he was in the dark woods. The thought of letting his tiger take him made him feel better already. As he moved deeper into the wooded area, he pushed aside all thoughts of his work life, the woman, and everything else that didn't have to do with where he was and what he was doing right now. Leaping forward, he shifted into his cat even before he hit the ground running.

He had no idea how long he'd been out there before he got back to his truck. The tree was out of the back end, as were the flats of flowers. When he picked up his phone, he saw that he had ten messages and figured if it was his family, they knew how to reach him. Pulling on his shirt and tie, he made his way to the house with the flowers he'd gotten for his mom. The butler told him that neither of his parents was home.

"Did they say where they were going?" He told him that they hadn't. "I wanted to talk to Mom. I don't suppose she said when they'd be home."

"No, sir. They did not. Mr. Harrison left at his usual time, but the missus left not long ago. She had the gardener take the things from your truck. Mrs. Harrison is not in the habit of leaving like she did, so I do hope there is nothing wrong."

Riordan did as well. Making his way to work after handing the flowers over, he reached out to his parents. His dad said that he was too busy to chat right now, and his mother told him she wasn't speaking to him. Riordan went to his office with a heavy heart. He didn't like his parents being upset with him. But his day was full, and he thought about going over there after work if he was able to get off early. He didn't anticipate that happening after having the morning off, but he was going to try. Even Christina wasn't at her desk when he arrived. This was going to be a shitty day all around.

# CHAPTER 3

The room was dark when she woke up, but Storm had a feeling that she wasn't alone. One of her aunts had to be with her, as they usually were when she had a bad time of it. Moving slowly so as not to wake them should they be resting, a moan escaped before she could stop it. The light flaring made her cry out; it had startled her into a small jump.

"I'm terribly sorry. I didn't think." Storm tried to see who it was that was speaking, as the voice didn't sound familiar. "I'm Briana Harrison, but most people call me Bri. I haven't the slightest idea why they do that, but Ordan does and that's all right with me. Why is that name all that much shorter than…? I'm sorry. Can I get you anything?"

"My aunts, where are they?" It even hurt to talk, so she cleared her throat a little and tried to sit up. "Where are they?"

"Your Aunt Lynn has gone to the store. She said that you were out of everything. I've looked. She's right. You can't live on just cereal. It's not good for you and—" Storm cleared her throat again. "Right. Where are they? Aunt Sally is counting out the drawer. She's been doing it for over two hours. I don't think she is good with money. I sent my husband to help her out. The credit card machine is giving her fits, she said."

"She forgets to send the money to the account nightly. I'm sure that's all it is." Storm was feeling slightly better and sat up a little more. "I don't know you, do I?"

"No. My husband is the man you...well, he helped you out the other day when he brought you up here."

Storm had no idea what she was talking about, then realized what she'd said. "Other day? How long have I been here?" Bri told her. "Three days? I've been unconscious for three days? What the fuck is she thinking?"

"I'm thinking she thought you needed it or you wouldn't have slept all this time. And don't you dare get out of that bed." Something about her tone had Storm pause in tossing the blanket off her. "Now. We're going to sit here and have a lovely conversation, you and me. I should explain to you who I am. I'm the idiot's mother. And while I don't normally think of Riordan as an idiot, I believe this time he was out of line."

"I know a lot of idiots, ma'am; perhaps you can narrow it down." The smile made her think of the man who had been in the day before...well, a few days ago. "You're Mac's mother. And the wife of the man...Mr. Harrison. I hurt him and he...my aunts spiked my ass and I fell into unconsciousness."

"Yes. That's right. He feels horrible for what he did to you. I've never met you before this, but I bet you don't go around pointing guns at men all the time. He startled you, that's all it was."

"Mrs. Harrison, I'm armed all the time." Storm pushed her hand up under the pillow she was on and pulled out a gun, then laid it on her lap. "In this room alone, there are four of them. Two in the kitchen area and one in my bathroom. In my cooking area, there are at least six, one under the counter in the front, and two in the dining area. It's not much of a dining area right now, but it will be if this business keeps up."

"Is it because you're afraid, or is it because of what happened to you when you were in the service?" Storm told her both. "I see. And when you pulled the gun on Ordan, did you have intentions of killing him or...or just frightening him?"

"I don't know." When Bri nodded and stood up, Storm stretched out her legs. She was going to have to get up soon or she'd stiffen up to the point where she'd need help getting out of the bed. Right now it was iffy if she was going to be able to stand after being down for three days. "I'm going to have to move soon. I don't want to be rude, but I have to get up and into the shower."

"Can I help you?" Storm told her to not touch her. "You're very rude. I'm thinking you and Riordan will suit better than I thought. Would it hurt you to say please or thank you once in a while?" Her smile made Storm think that while she was more than likely serious in her request, she wasn't really upset about it.

"Who is Riordan? Oh, the idiot. I don't want him to touch me either. I hurt in too many places for touching to be possible." Storm sat on the edge of her bed and counted to ten while she let out a low breath. It was what she'd learned to do when the doctors at the hospital in country had told her she'd never walk again without assistance. The blanket was still over her legs, but she'd have to get rid of that to walk. The woman was going to get an eyeful if she was still around when she got up. "I'm not...I've been hurt badly. When I stand up...if I manage to stand up, you're going to wish you'd left a while ago."

"Why is that?" Storm pulled the blanket from her body. Few people saw her this way, and she thought that the only ones who had seen her entire body had been the doctors and nurses. She'd not looked herself...it was just too much. "Oh, you poor girl."

For reasons that she couldn't explain, Storm didn't want to lash out at the woman. She'd had people say the same thing to her before, nurses who hadn't been around her much. Doctors that had thought to come by her bed and see if they could reason with her. Storm didn't do reason. She was someone who got things done. But Mrs. H sounded sincere in her sorrow. When she came closer to her, Storm pulled the blanket back over herself.

"They thought they were going to have to take them off. From the knees down. The doctor told me afterwards that they still might have to, but then I started to walk. I'm not one to give up easily." Bri said she could see that. "The bones are weak still and there is a lot of muscle damage that might not ever heal, but I move around now and that's enough for me."

"I read about it. Not who you were…the papers kept that out of the news. I wasn't sure why until I talked to your aunts. They said that because of what you were in the service, they were keeping it quiet. That you were more than just a soldier." Storm didn't say anything as Bri continued. "She told me what you did while you were hanging there, too. She told me that they found you in a tree. I'm sorry."

"I don't know who told her that, but that's not for…I would appreciate it if you said nothing about that." Bri nodded and sat down. "I'm hoping you can see now why your son shouldn't pursue this any further. I'm not really the type of woman he should be dating, much less taking as a mate."

"I don't know why you'd think that." Storm nodded to her legs. "I'm sure that the two of you got off on the wrong foot. Riordan has been…I'm not sure what's been wrong with him of late, but he didn't do well with you. But as far as what you've been through, I'm sure that it will matter little to him what you look like so long as you're happy."

"But I'm not. Happy." Storm stood up and held onto the wall near her bed until she thought she could move. "I'm really sorry about this. But I'd really be grateful if you told your son to stay away. I know that so long as there is no contact with us sexually, or that he never takes my blood, he should be fine. But this is not something I want. Not now and not ever."

Bri didn't say anything, but she did follow her to the bathroom. When she reached into the stall and turned on the water, Bri asked her if she needed anything before she left. After telling her that she was fine, the woman left her and Storm stripped down. Without looking in the mirror that hung over the sink, Storm got into the shower. Closing her eyes as she usually did when naked, she scrubbed her body until it ached.

Dressing wasn't usually so difficult. Pulling on a pair of jeans took her ten minutes longer than it should have. Not even bothering with shoes and socks, she moved to the closet and pulled out the first shirt she touched. They were all the same anyway...dark with no pockets, and too long even for her tall body. Pulling it over her head, she made her way to the stairs. Going down them had always been a scary job, but today it was positively terrifying. As she got to the bottom, Storm stood there for several seconds just to get her heartbeat under control again. Her Aunt Lynn was the first person she saw.

"Well, look who's up and about. I was going to bring some food up for you later. What can I make you to eat?" Storm told her she wasn't hungry. "Well, too bad. I'm going to make you something and you're going to eat it. You can pick or I can make you something I like."

"A sandwich. But I really am not hungry. I'm...I hurt." Aunt Lynn told her that she knew and kissed her on the cheek as she moved by her to the large refrigerator.

Aunt Sally came into the kitchen with a cash bag and receipts. She looked like she'd been run through the ringer.

"That nice Mr. Harrison helped me out, but I don't want to have to do that again. I was over six hundred dollars in the hole until he showed up. Then poof, there it was." Storm was terrified to think that they'd only made that much in the three days that she'd been down. At this rate, they'd be lucky if they made it for another two months. "Yesterday wasn't so bad. But Mrs. Harrison did the paperwork then. And Lynn did it the first time. You're going to be happy to know that I'm quitting as the cashier, too. Those things scare the beeswax out of me."

"I've heard the word shit a few times, Aunt Sally." She huffed at her and sat down across from her. "How has Danny been working out? Or has he stopped coming?"

"Danny has been here every day and is doing a fine job. And we hired another man that came by, too." Aunt Lynn sat beside her and put a sandwich and chips with a large glass of tea in front of her as Aunt Sally continued. "Mr. Harrison interviewed him for us. Such a nice man. Did you know that he and his wife have been helping us out, too? Bri, we're to call her that, she's been trying her hand at baking. And she's done a fine job, but I think she and Ordan have had the most fun working the front for us. Lynn and I have been baking things and then selling them, too. I forgot how much fun it was. But I can see why you took it over for us. It's a lot of hard work for a couple of old women."

"Neither of you is old. I'm really sorry that I had to put you through this. I hope you kept track of what they worked. I need to pay them, too." Aunt Lynn shook her head. "Yes, I do. I don't know how well we did, but we can't owe people like them money."

"You did very well. Extremely well, as a matter of fact. And we kept track of the hours and, believe it or not, they only wanted pastries in trade. Ordan has a real sweet tooth, and Bri wanted breads for her Sunday dinners with her family." Storm was looking over the books for the last three days and looked at Aunt Lynn.

"Is this right?" She nodded and smiled. "We made twenty grand in three days? What the hell were you selling that was worth that much?"

"Well, it's not all pastries. Your aunt and I did a few tricks on the side. It was sort of fun, but men are such pigs." Storm stared at her with wide eyes until she laughed. "You should see your face. No, it's not that. We sold that old cabinet in the back, the one you wanted to use as a display. The man gave you eight thousand for it. I know that I should have asked, but he made us a deal. We can go to his shop and get some tables and chairs for out front, and he'll sell them to us for half price."

"What kind of shop?" Her aunts said they'd been there and it was nice. "An antique shop? And he just happens to have tables and chairs for us?"

"Yes. Why are you always so suspicious of people, darling?" Storm didn't say anything, but they seemed to understand. "We're going to go over there tonight and pick out five sets if he has them. That way when our customers want to have a seat, we can let them."

Storm didn't tell them to be careful. Her aunts might be elderly, and they might seem a little off at times, but neither of them would be taken advantage of, and no one would pull the wool over their eyes. If the man was thinking to take them for a ride, he was going to be in for a huge surprise. Her aunts were as crafty as they came, and not the glitter and glue kind.

~~~

Riordan had been summoned home. He wasn't sure what was going on, but he knew better than to tell them he was too busy. When he told his dad that it would take him a little bit to have Christina clear his morning, his dad told him to clear the day. Whatever was going on, he wasn't happy with him. Riordan thought about getting another dozen roses to take to Mom, but thought she might shove them in his face.

Christina had told him just before she'd left yesterday that she had the information on The Bakery. Then she'd asked him if he read the article that she'd sent him. He told her that he'd forgotten about it. For the rest of the day, she only left him notes if she wanted him to know something, and then when he had to talk to her, she was short and ill-tempered. There had to be something going on that no one had told him about. And just as he was pulling up the link she'd sent him, his dad had called to tell him to come home. Now.

His mom led him to the living room, a room that was warm and comfortable usually, but today felt frosty. His mom asked him to have a seat. When he was seated, she told him how disappointed she was in him.

"In me? What did I do?" She looked at his dad, and so did he. "I've been working. And if this is about that woman, I want you to know how sorry I am that I embarrassed you with this. I've been trying to figure out how to tell her I'm sorry, too, but she's been out of the shop. I honestly don't think I did anything wrong with her, but I'm going to apologize to her so you won't be mad at me."

"She was hurt when she pulled a gun on me. I didn't mean to startle her. It was entirely my fault, but she was hurting and I felt terrible about it. Even more after I was told what had happened to her. You should know that you hurt her, too, when you jumped at her."

Riordan felt the roaring in his head when his dad said gun. He was standing up when his mom barked at him to sit. Riordan nearly missed the chair when he sat down, but he was as hot as he could be about this shit. She was going to pay for this. And pay dearly.

"What do you plan to do, Riordan? Go down there and demand that she tell you what she was thinking when your father just told you it was his fault? Will you shoot her, maybe? Make her mad at you before you get all the facts?" He glared at his mom, and she glared back. "You can take that look off your face right now, before I make you regret it."

"She tried to shoot Dad and you're defending her?" He looked at his dad as he continued. "What the hell is she doing with a gun anyway? Is that how she gets what she wants from people? Is that why you're thinking of investing in her little shop, because she's using extortion?"

"She's a vet. A wounded vet who nearly died less than two years ago while fighting for our country." That had him leaning back in his chair, and anything that might have spilled from his mouth felt like bile in his throat. His mom sat down, her voice low now that she was upset. And she was. He could see that now. "I've seen her. Her legs. And her aunts told me what little they know of what happened to her. Her commanding officer only told them a little, and Storm tells them nothing is wrong, of course. I've talked to her, and I think she believes she's protecting them."

"Protecting them from what?" She said she didn't know. "I don't understand what this has to do with her pulling a gun on Dad. What the hell was she thinking?"

"She wasn't. Thinking, I mean. And as I said, it's more my fault than hers." He asked him how. "I went there that day to see her. To tell her...to tell her that we'd raised you better than you'd acted before. But the shop was busy, and Lynn told me to go on back to see her. She was in the kitchen at the table when I got there. It never occurred to me that she was asleep, so I touched her arm. Just as a warning that I was there so as not to startle her from her work."

"And she tried to kill you." Riordan got up to pace. "She's a vet, I get that, but what the hell was she doing with a gun? I mean, really?"

"Here. I was given this to read." His mom handed him a sheaf of papers. "Read this. It doesn't say her name because of her ranking in the service or something like that, her aunt told me. But it does tell what happened over the two days that left her in the pain that she's in. And I'm talking real pain, the kind that would cripple most people."

Riordan held the papers and looked around the room at his parents' home before speaking. Having them defend her was beyond anything he would have thought they'd do. And the fact that they were blowing off this thing with the gun so casually pissed him off, too. Riordan stood to leave. "You do know that this means nothing to me. She hurt you and she's going to—"

"Shut up and sit down." His father never raised his voice. Not when they were children and not since Riordan had been an adult. But he did now, and Riordan sat down. He watched as his dad paced the room much the same as he had. "When did you become so cold, son? And you are. Cold as a stone.

39

And why? This girl has done nothing to you. She's been telling us to keep you away from her since we been helping her. And yes, before you get yourself all pissed off again, we have been helping her. We've been running the shop with her aunts. Your mom has been baking a little. And we've had fun getting to know her aunts. Her great aunts, as a matter of fact. I was called a young man. Imagine that…someone thinking of me as a young man. And I had fun. We both did. Now read the damned papers. This isn't like you to be so…so halfcocked about something."

He was left in the room alone. The ticking of the grandfather clock near the fireplace was the only sound in the big room. Riordan didn't want to read about some phantom person who may or may not be the woman who had pulled a gun on his dad. But he knew that he'd better or he'd face the wrath of his parents again.

Starting at the headline, Riordan laughed. Someone had made this shit up, he thought. Humvee Massacre Results in Best Intel. But by the second paragraph he was trying to fit the girl that he'd met briefly to the story that was being told. And by the time he was on the third page of the long article, Riordan knew that not only had he been wrong about the woman, but about nearly everything he'd been thinking about her as his mate, too. She was a bigger and better person than he was or ever would be. By the time he read the last line, where the person who wrote it explained why there was no mention of a name because of security reasons, he felt like a real shit. Riordan went to find his mom in the kitchen.

"Your dad was called away. He wanted to be here when you finished, but something has come up. Did you read it?" He nodded and sat down with her. "And do you still think she's this horrible person only out to harm us?"

"I honestly don't know what to think now. How do you know this is her? I mean, it's a horrific story, but how do you know this is her and not someone else? As you've said, there is no mention of her name."

His mom got up and poured him a cup of hot tea. He watched her, knowing that she was working out in her head how to answer him. Riordan wanted to ask her to just say it, but he knew that she'd not be able to do that anymore than he could have.

"The article came to me from Mac. He said he pulled some strings when he figured out who she was. Mac said that he'd heard her name, a while ago, in a conversation he'd been having with his friend, that guy in the service, Blackson. He's high up on the ranking order, I think. He went to talk to him." She sat down and sipped her tea before continuing. "Mac told him what she was to you and asked him to confirm or deny who she was. He said that not only was this her, but she's still considered active and will have the full pay and ranking for as long as she lives. The president has made it perfectly clear that not only did she save hundreds of men that day, but without her observations and help when it came to a covert operation, the war would have taken a terrible turn."

"What did she do?" Mom shrugged and sipped her tea again. "This thing with Dad, she was asleep and she attacked him. Why? Do you know that?"

"Yes." When she said nothing else, he asked her what she knew. "I'm sorry, son, but I'm not going to tell you everything I know, which I might add, is not a great deal. What I will tell you is this. She's been living with her aunts since she was released a few months ago. The aunts own the building that the bakery is now in, and decided that they wanted to add to their pension some and opened the bakery with her help. I don't know why she lives above the place when I know from them that she has a house somewhere near here. I don't know, other than the damage done to her legs, what else was done to her or how she was hurt, other than what you've read there."

"She's my mate." Mom nodded and smiled at him. "Why do I get the feeling that you're enjoying this? I don't know what this is, but you're having a good time with it."

"I am. You have met your match, son. And I don't mean just your mate. Storm is strong-willed, strong-minded, and she's smart. She'll have you in knots so tight that you won't know which way is up." Mom stood up, taking both of their now-empty cups to the counter to rinse out. She turned to continue. "But she will love you like no one else ever will, protect you in ways that you can't her, and there will never be a time when you think that she's not the right person for you, when you give her half a chance."

"That's the problem right there. I don't want to be tied up. Not over a woman, and I don't want to have to worry about whether or not she's going to pull a gun on the next person that touches her. I have my life just the way I like it. A nice bank account. I was dating a woman that, while I know she's not my mate, she did suit me. And a job that I love." He stood up then and kissed his mom on the cheek. "I'm going to leave her where she is. We've not touched each other except for that one time, and I have no intentions of going back there to see her again. As far as I'm concerned, she can live in her little part of the world and I can live in mine."

"You really think it's going to work like that?" He told her that it was going to have to. "Well, then I wish you the best of luck with that. But I like her and her aunts. I'm going to continue to see her. Go to her shop and work a little if she'll let me. And whether you like it or not, I'm going to have her here for dinner sometimes. If you would rather be left out of those family times, then I can arrange that, too."

Riordan left a little while later. He was hot, and he was pretty sure his mom knew it. This was the stupidest thing he'd ever had happen to him, and his parents were taking the side of a stranger. A human stranger, as a matter of fact. Driving to his apartment complex, he parked in the garage and sat there for ten minutes before he started cursing. Starting up his truck again, he made his way to The Bakery to have a word or two with Storm Browning.

# CHAPTER 4

"Stormy, that man is here again. The idiot." Aunt Lynn came more into the room with her and leaned into her ear. "He's not any happier about being here than I am having him here. And so you know, Sally is giving him what for."

Storm could have told her to toss him out, but she was pretty sure that her aunt would. Right out on the front walk and then clap her hands about it. Instead of making more trouble for them and herself, she moved to the front of the shop just as one of the men from the VA hospital came in the door. This could not be good.

Pointing to Riordan, she told him to stand right where he was and went to deal with Doctor Keller. The man had been calling here for two weeks, and she'd had about all she could take of him. When he put out his hand to shake hers, Storm just stared at it until he dropped it.

"You were told to keep your distance." The man actually grinned at her. "And by distance, it was supposed to be over one hundred yards. This is less than a few feet. Even you should know the difference."

"You missed an appointment. Again." Storm said nothing but knew that Riordan had come up behind her. "Hello. I'm Doctor Andy Keller. The sergeant major here has missed a few appointments at the hospital where she's being treated."

"Is that so?" Riordan put out his hand for the doctor, and Storm had to cover a laugh when Andy winced from the

43

obvious tight grip that Riordan was giving him. "What are you treating her for?"

"I'm not at liberty to say. But I will say this…she must attend the meetings or she'll be in trouble." Riordan asked him if they were meetings or appointments. "Meetings. Why does that matter?"

"What sort of meetings? Something she's, I don't know, required to go to pending some sort of firing?" He said no, they weren't like that. "So, who else is in this meeting? I'm assuming that since she just said that she has an order with someone that you have to stay away from her, that it's not with you."

"No, it's a group meeting. Another doctor is running these meetings. I'm doing him a favor by coming by and checking on her. The meetings are where she talks about her feelings and what she's been going through. It's to help her with some of the stress that she could be dealing with. All vets should come to meetings like that."

Riordan nodded and looked at her before speaking. "I've not known Storm for that long, but I'm pretty sure that if she had a problem, she'd tell you straight out. And if she had a problem, I'm betting she can fix it a good deal faster than you could. Or this doctor friend you have." Riordan pulled out his cell phone. "I tell you what, you give me his phone number and I'll explain to him just why you can't come here anymore. And that sending you here on a fool's errand like he did is going to get your ass and his kicked all over this pretty little restaurant."

"Are you threatening me? I'll have you know that I work for the United States government, and I will not be—"

"I'm not going to do a damned thing to you. I'm talking about her. I'm pretty sure that— like I said, not knowing her well—but I'm pretty sure that she can use your ass to mop up this floor and not even break a nail doing it." They both looked at her, and she stretched her neck. The popping sound had Andy backing up two steps. "Did you know that's she more than likely armed? I mean, right this minute?"

"I've come down here as a favor to—"

"You tell that lie again and I will shoot what I'm sure is that tiny dick of yours off." Cupping himself, Andy backed more away from her. "If you come here again, bother me with one more phone call, I'm going to call Brigadier General Blackson. Do you remember what he said to you the last time I called him?"

Without a word, Andy turned and left. The door to the bakery was still rattling when she turned to Riordan. He was grinning at her like he knew something about her that she didn't. Which was impossible…she knew her own self better than he ever thought he would.

"Look, Mr. Harrison, I'm very busy today. If you've come down here to blast me again, I would suggest that you leave now while you can. I'm neither in the mood to fuck around with you today or fight." He started to reach for her when she turned, and Storm backed out of his touch. "Don't. Don't touch me."

"All right. For now." She had no idea what he meant but moved to the back room again. She really was busy and didn't want to get even more behind than she already was. He was right behind her when she stopped at the board again. Turning, she backed up when he was simply too close.

"What the fuck do you want?" Her head was hurting, and her back was throbbing like someone was standing on it doing a jig. "I thought I made it perfectly clear that you're not welcome here. And from my understanding, you want less to do with me than I do with you. Which is saying a great deal."

"What did he really want? The doctor. What did he really want you to do?"

She thought about telling him to fuck off, but only shook her head. What would be the point? He wasn't going to leave until he had everything answered. And she was simply too tired and too sore to fight with him over it at the moment.

"He has it in his head that we're going to be an item, and I'm going to somehow advance his career. That I'm going to get him in good with the president. I think, at least I hope, the president has more sense than to want that fool as his personal physician. He can't keep his hands to himself, and he thinks that I'm just too lonely to turn him down. I'm not lonely, I'm busy, as I have told you several times already today." She walked away from him when he turned to look toward the front of the building.

"You think that's all he wants from you?" She asked him what else he thought the man wanted as she picked up fifty pounds of flour. Riordan took it from her and asked her if she needed more.

"Yes. I need three bags. But I'm capable of picking them up all by myself. I'm a big girl, in the event that escaped your notice." He only grunted at her and picked up the other two that she was going to have to come back for. "I really wish you'd say whatever it is you want and get out of here. I'm sporting a fucker of a headache and I don't want to keep trying to be nice to you."

"You were being nice?" She glared at him, and he grinned. Storm turned away from him. The man was simply too charming when he wanted to be. "I came here because…actually, I have no idea why I came here today. To talk to you for one thing. And to try and settle things between us."

"There is no *us,* and *we* have nothing to settle." Measuring out the flour that she needed, she looked at the next item on her list and wondered if she could make the two batches together. "I don't want to have any sort of relationship with anyone. I've got my life all mapped out and believe it or not, Mr. Harrison, you're not even a blip on my list. Go away."

"I've been thinking."

She started to ask him if it was painful but didn't. Her head was killing her, and she just wanted it quiet for a while.

Danny came from the sinks and cleared his throat. He was the quietest man she knew.

"I got Brady all trained now. I don't think he's going to work out though. He's got himself a complex, and he's gonna act on it soon. Today if I don't miss my bet. I would like to talk to you about his...." Danny looked pointedly at Riordan and shrugged. "He's got some problems."

"Like?" She was sick to death of the cat-and-mouse games that people played. "Spill it, soldier. I have a long list of shit that I have to do, and you're taking up my space. And this ass is going to be leaving soon, too."

Danny grinned at her, just like she knew he would. "He's supposed to be on some of those anti-depressing shit. But he's not popping them right. And he has himself an issue." She asked him if it was a service issue and he told her no. "Told me that he got it off a friend of his and that he was tired of just making it by. I'm thinking he's on a short one. You should maybe make a call. He was telling me that taking himself out a hero and all was going to get him noticed. Might be that he's talking about popping you."

"Fucking newspaper just had to talk about the new bakery and mention my name. Where is he?" He told her in the pantry putting away the stuff that just came in. Storm looked at Riordan and tried to think past the pounding right behind her eyes. She looked at Danny and nodded to Riordan. "Take him up front with my aunts. I'm going to talk to him. Lock up and down, understand?"

Danny told her he did and moved toward Riordan. But he was shaking his head even before Danny tried to ask him to come along. "I'm not leaving you. I don't know half the crap you just said, but I don't think you're safe."

"It means for him to lock up the front door and to keep his fucking head down between his legs. And I am safe; you're not. Go to the front with Danny." He told her no. "Fuck. You know, I really don't need this right now. My head hurts like a son of a bitch. You're irritating the shit out of me, and I have a kid here that wants to be killed by cops by taking me out. What the fuck else could possibly go wrong today?"

"Plenty I'm sure, but I'm not leaving you."

Storm picked up the phone then and called the police. It wasn't really the right order to do things, but there were civilians in her place, and they had to come first. Pulling out her gun when she hung up, she looked at Riordan.

"You get shot and I'm going to be really pissed." He asked her what he could do. "Will you go up front? If not, then I need for you to stay out of the way and don't fucking move when he comes out. Do you understand me?"

"Is he going to shoot you?" She told him probably. "I can't let that happen. You're my mate, and I have to protect you."

"Are you faster than a bullet? I'm thinking not, but if you are, then by all means, take point on this. But if you want to keep me safe, then stay the fuck out of my way. I know what I'm doing." He nodded but didn't look happy about it. Storm turned to the pantry. "Brady? It's Storm Browning. Can you come out here?"

~~~

Riordan called his mom, then his dad. He thought about just contacting them through his link with them, but he was scared out of his ever-loving fucking mind and needed to talk to them personally. When his mom hung up, he called his dad. He told him everything that happened, too.

"Oh my God, son. Is anyone hurt? You? Are you hurt?" He told him that he wasn't. "And Stormy, is she…did she get hurt?"

"She was shot at, but the man she was talking to, he's dead. She had to kill him or…she saved my life." His dad said that he was on his way. That he was only at the office. "Mom is coming, too. Ennis is driving her."

"Good, that's good. I'm walking. I don't think I could drive. And you're all right, you promise me that?" He told his dad that he really was fine. "I'm…you have no idea what is running through my mind right now. You're okay, son, right?"

"I am, Dad, I promise you I am. Storm is fine, too. Shook up, but the man with her is talking to her. She said she has a headache, and he said he was going to have her checked out at the hospital. I don't think she's all that thrilled about that." Dad said that he could see her being upset about someone wanting to care of her. "She shot him, Dad. Right between the eyes when he…he was going to kill me, then her. I was told to stay out of the way, and I didn't. I think she could have been able to talk him down if not for me being there."

"I'm here, son; come out and tell them I can come to you."

He closed his phone and went to the front of the bakery. Sally and Lynn were handing out coffee and Danish to anyone that wanted them, and he was pretty sure to a few people that didn't. Danny was talking to someone in a uniform, but it wasn't police. He looked at him and nodded but continued talking. As soon as he saw his dad, he was pulled into a great bear hug that Riordan hadn't realized he needed until just then.

He led him to the back where there were more uniforms than he'd seen on Memorial Day. All of them were wearing stripes up and down on their sleeves, and a few of them were sporting stars and bars on their collars. Mac was there with his friend, Tony Blackson, and the latter was talking to Storm. It didn't sound like he was having any more luck with her than the doctor had been earlier.

"Just go down to the hospital and let them check you out, that's all I'm asking." She growled at the man, and Riordan had to hide a smile. But she must have heard him and looked right at him.

He expected her to tell them this was his fault. It sort of had been. When Brady had come out of the pantry, he'd been pointing the gun right at her. Storm had hers at her side. Riordan didn't move even when Brady asked what he was doing there. But his cat wasn't very happy with the situation. Riordan remembered every word that was exchanged between her and this Brady person. Brady had asked her again what he was doing there.

"He's here to see me. For what, I couldn't tell you. He's a pain in my ass, too. What the fuck are you doing? Do you have any idea what I am to you?"

He said "Yes, sir" like it had been drilled in his head to do so from birth.

"So you must have a good excuse for doing this then. What the hell is it? You want me to shoot you? Because as I see things right now, you're pointing a weapon at a superior officer. Is that the way they're teaching you grunts to do things now?"

"No, sir, they don't teach us that. But I'm just tired." She told him she was, too. "My head is all messed up. I got me thoughts in there that I don't care for. And I don't know how to get them done with."

"You're not taking your meds, are you?" He told her he didn't like how they made him feel. "Well, tough fucking shit, you moron, that's what you're supposed to do to feel better. I don't like having a gun pointed at me either. So I guess we neither one are getting what we want, now are we?"

"Maybe if I kill you, then I can just go about my business like before." She asked him how the hell he thought that was going to work. "I don't know. Like I was before they took me over there. I had to kill people, and when I get back here, they say I can't do that anymore. But I just couldn't help it. She made me do it."

Brady had pointed the gun at Riordan, and Storm stepped in front of it, telling him he didn't want to do that. Riordan reached for Storm to move her, but before he could get her out of the way, Brady had knocked Storm to the table and had Riordan by the neck with the gun pointed to his head.

"I'm going to kill you both." She told him no he wasn't. "I am. I'm going to kill him, then you. I can. I've done it before. I got me no problems with this. You'll see, it'll be over soon."

Storm lifted her gun and told him to drop his. When he told her no, the next thing Riordan knew he found himself being helped up from his knees and Brady was dead on the floor. Storm told him to stand back when he moved toward the younger man. And that was when the police showed up.

It was iffy for a few minutes as to whether or not they were going to shoot her, or at the very least arrest her. But Blackson had shown up with Mac and everyone got an earful from Blackson. In a few minutes there were no police allowed within a foot of him or Storm, and Blackson was clearly in charge. The man wasn't happy, and for some reason, Riordan didn't think it was because the man on the floor was dead.

Mac pulled him aside when Blackson asked for a moment with his soldier. Riordan didn't want to leave her, and it surprised him that the reason he didn't was because he didn't care for Blackson. Riordan moved away but kept her in his sights. He looked at Mac when he laughed.

"Mom is out front. She wants to know if you want her to stay with Stormy while you go to the office to work." He started to ask him what he was talking about when he continued. "I think they're under the impression that you don't want her as your mate. It looks to me like if you had your way, she'd be in bed with you between her legs. Or am I wrong?"

His dad saved him from having to answer, or kill Mac. He was having entirely too much fun at his expense. Everyone seemed to be doing that lately. He moved out to his mom, and she was standing next to Storm. Riordan moved closer to hear what the yelling was about.

"You'll do this or so help me, I'm going to be very upset with you." Storm asked her if it would be more than she was now. "You bet your bottom dollar it will be. I will tear your bottom up, and then you'll have something worth going to the hospital about."

51

"I don't think that makes the least bit of sense." Storm looked at him. "Is she always like this? Bossy to the point of you wanting to strangle her?"

"I'm not going to answer that." He winked at her. "You're very beautiful when you're pissed off, aren't you?"

He felt everyone turn to look at him, but for some reason, he didn't really care what they thought of him at that moment. This woman…his woman…had done something that no one else had ever done. She'd stood up to a man with a gun and had saved his life. But he wasn't stupid enough to think that she'd not shoot him too should he piss her off more.

In the end, his mom bullied her into going. Storm stopped talking to him and his mom, but she did talk to Blackson. Apparently, Danny had called him the moment she'd had them go to the front of the shop. And it was a good thing, too. She wasn't going to jail for what had happened today.

Blackson grabbed him just before he was ready to go to his truck and follow the ambulance. He'd known that the man wasn't human. He was a wolf, and more than likely Storm knew what he was as well. But when he took him in the pantry and closed the door, Riordan felt his cat stir along his skin.

"She's not going to come to you easily. You know that, right?" Riordan just nodded. "There is something else you should know. It's not…she's…I'm not sure how to say this without you leaping at my throat."

"Just say it." The man nodded but didn't speak. Riordan had all sorts of things running through his head. She was married. There were fifty kids in her life. The thoughts were going to be much worse than what it really was, he knew that, but he was still nervous. "I may attack now if you don't spill it."

"When Stormy entered the service after turning eighteen, I was brought her test scores. They were off the charts. I mean, she's got an IQ that most of them who work in the labs around the country would kill for. I immediately went to meet her." He grinned at him. "As you can well imagine, that didn't go over as well as I'd hoped. If you think she's smart mouthed now, you should have seen her before we trained her. Caustic doesn't even begin to tell you the way she spoke. But like I said, we trained her. It didn't take much. Her intelligence alone was enough to keep us hopping, and her ability to adapt to any situation was what made her into the kind of soldier we needed and still need. She can speak nine languages fluently, and several more just in passing. She hears it once, just one time, and she can speak it back flawlessly. She worked for and still does work for a very covert group of men and women that come in and take charge when negotiations have all but failed."

"I'm not sure why you think I need to know this now. I would really like to go to make sure she's all right." Blackson nodded but didn't look like he was ready to release him just yet. "What is it you're trying your best not to tell me?"

"My plan had been to convert her. You'll see by her medical records that she was to have her leg taken off...both of them, actually. She has some ribs that will never heal, and she'll be in a great deal of pain for the rest of her life. By all accounts, Stormy should have died that day. And if not the day of the accident, then while she hung there in that tree." Riordan asked him what he meant. "She's not told you. Well, that's no surprise. I'm not sure she's even shared with her aunts. But when the Humvee blew up, Stormy was tossed from the accident and into a tree. She hung there for thirty-six hours, with a branch through her holding her in place. Its...she could see from above what our surveillance couldn't."

Riordan tried to equate what he was telling him with the woman he knew. "You mean, she stood on a branch."

"No. It entered her here." He turned and showed him his back, just below the ribs. "Then came out here." He then put his hand over his chest, just below his heart.

"That's not possible." Blackson told him he knew that, yet she'd survived it. "My mom said that her legs were scarred up. That her muscles are…they're spent, she thought."

"I don't know if I'd risk changing her, Riordan. She's weak and her body will more than likely not take it well. There is a possibility, and not a slim one, that she will not survive any kind of trauma to her body. She's held together by bubble gum and string. Not really, but she is fragile." Riordan nodded. "I'm not one to usually beat around the bush, and now that I can tell you're not going to kill me, be as gentle as your cat will allow you when you have sex with her, too. She's in constant pain, and it won't take much to send her into unconsciousness."

He left then, and Riordan drove to the hospital with his mom beside him. Dad was following in his car to bring Mom home should he want to stay with Storm. When she touched his arm after they parked, he looked at her. His thoughts on Blackson were making him crazy. There was something about the man that he just didn't like. He supposed it was because he was so close to her, and Riordan wasn't.

"I'm such a fool." His mom said nothing but just watched him. "She's been telling me no, not because she didn't want me but because she thinks I'm not going to want her. Right? That's why she's been shoving me away and not letting me get close to her. I've…I'm such a fool."

"Her aunts think if she were to tell someone what really happened she'd start to heal. Not her body, but her mind. She has horrific nightmares sometimes. That's why she's living at the shop and not in her house. When she wakes, she goes down to bake something."

Riordan nodded, knowing that he did the same thing on some level when he couldn't sleep. "I'll try, Mom. But I need to fix this with her first." She nodded. "Any suggestions?"

"Yes. Grovel. Works for me when your dad has to do it. Not often, but he still does." He nodded. How did you grovel to a woman that carried a gun, would just as soon murder you than let you touch her, and worked for an agency that had trained her to kill rather than to negotiate? He was so fucked.

# CHAPTER 5

Storm watched the monitors that had been attached to her when she arrived. Not that she minded them that much…she just hated having to sit still for them to work. When the door opened again, it was on the tip of her tongue to blast Blackson again for doing this to her. Only it wasn't him but Bri Harrison.

"You were going to say something entirely unladylike, weren't you?" Storm felt her face heat up, and Bri laughed. "I love that I can catch you off guard. I bet it doesn't happen very often. May I ask who you thought was coming in?"

"Blackson. He said he had something for me to…something he needed for me to look at." Bri sat down and smiled at her. "If I asked you to leave, you wouldn't do it, would you?"

"No. Not yet. I was told that you're going to be upset in a few minutes and I want to be here to see it. It's not often that Riordan is in over his head. And with you, I think he is." Storm started to tell her that he'd not be in over his head if he just left her alone, but Bri continued. "I was scared out of my mind when he called me. I knew that he'd been frightened but not why. And when his phone call came through to me, I nearly didn't want to answer it. I owe you a great deal for saving his life."

"He wouldn't have had to be saved if he had just done what I told him." Bri nodded and then smiled at her. "I can see where he gets his supposed charm. You. He thinks that if he just smiles a little, things will go the way he wants them to. Or demands them to. I'm not swayed by charm or his good looks. I'm over that shit."

"Yes, that's him, but I don't think you're as over it, as you say, as you might think. And the charming part is not something that most would call him. Mac is charming. You've met him. And I think that Aedan is as well, but he's a romantic more than just simply charming. You've not met the others, have you?" Storm told her no and leaned back on the bed. The monitor was hyping up, and that meant she'd be on it longer. Slowing her heart, she tried to concentrate on the woman's voice rather than what had happened today. "Tell me what happened."

"He stopped taking his meds. Two weeks ago. I don't know the entire story of why he was on them, and even if I did, I'd not share with you. But he was depressed. He told me that he hated the way they made him feel. I know what he meant. You feel sort of leggy and doped up." The door opened and closed, but she didn't open her eyes. When her IV was touched, Storm didn't think anything about it. It was a hospital after all. "When he had Riordan in his arms, all I could think about was you. I know that you think that's really stupid, but you were forefront and center. I didn't want to have to explain to you why he'd been killed."

"I can't thank you enough for that." Her voice sounded sort of sluggish, and Storm opened her eyes to look at the person touching her. The nurse standing there had a needle and she was pushing something into her IV site. Storm tried to ask her what it was, but Bri continued talking. "The entire family is grateful for it, too. Stormy, are you all right?"

Something was wrong. Something…she looked at Bri and noticed that she was waving in and out of focus. The nurse…it was all she could think about. Reaching behind her for her gun, Storm realized it was gone, taken for evidence. Grabbing for the nurse, her fingers slipped off her, and she looked at Bri as she pulled the needle from the IV. It was their only hope.

"Stop her."

The door slammed open and she heard a growl. As she felt herself slipping off into la-la land, Storm saw the big wolf, then the cat. Things were blurring in and out then, and she knew that whatever was going on, she could not help.

~~~

Riordan held Storm's hand as the men in the room cleaned up. They had thought to move her to another room, but Blackson said that would be a bad idea. So the blood and the body were being removed, as well as any evidence of what the nurse had been doing. Riordan looked at his mom as she sat there as calm as ever.

"She knew something was wrong and warned me." Riordan nodded and looked down at Storm when his mom spoke. "Why on earth would they hurt her here? Not that I think they should hurt her anywhere, but why?"

The IV that was running in her arm was not dripping like he'd seen them do, but running full tap, as Ennis had told him. It was pumping her system clean of the poison that had been given to her. Lucky for Storm, she'd pulled the needle out before more than a few drams of the stuff had been put in her. He was just glad that he and Blackson were so near when he said that Storm was in trouble. Riordan's opinion about the man had been wrong, he thought now.

His dad came in the room again and sat next to his mom. He was upset, too, but he was nicer about it.

The scrubs Riordan had been given felt foreign to him. After his suit clothes and shoes had been torn up when he shifted, Ennis had been nice enough to find him something to wear. He wasn't used to being so informal. And being uncomfortable wasn't helping his temper right now.

"If they hadn't made her come here, she'd be safe at her house." He tried his best to calm his cat, but he wanted to find the woman that had hurt Storm and kill her again. "I would think they'd listen to her when she says she's just fine."

The door opened again, and he had to fight hard with his other self not to shift and kill. And seeing Blackson didn't calm him either. Riordan felt his body crawling with the need to protect her when she was hurt like this, and Blackson seemed to know it. He stayed as far from the bed as he could without leaving the room.

"While I'm going to share what happened, I must tell you that sharing this information will have you before a firing squad. Anything and everything about today is going to be classified. But as her family, I'm going to bend the rules a little and let you know what happened." Riordan nodded, and so did his mom and dad. "First of all, the shooting at the bakery is going to be listed as a robbery gone wrong. He came in to get money for drugs and he was shot and killed by an unknown hero. Neither of you will be listed in any report filed, nor will anyone ever know that Stormy killed him because you were being held. Got that?"

"Why?" Riordan thought that a good question and nodded at his dad for asking it. Riordan had a lot more questions like that one, but he was willing to wait for answers one at a time. "Why not say that he came there depressed and wanted to commit suicide by cop?"

"Because it would have to be mentioned that Storm Browning was involved." Blackson sat down in the room's only other chair. Riordan looked at him then. The man was exhausted, and he'd bet that it had to do with this woman in front of him. "We're trying our best to keep her name...not just her name, but everything about her out of the paper. Sergeant Major Storm Browning is a name that would get her...as you can see, get her killed. She's a wanted woman in Afghanistan. Not for crimes that one would think, but crimes against their forces. They're saying that she is responsible for the murder of over nine hundred men, women, and children.

And in a way, she is. Just not the way that it is being broadcast in their neck of the woods."

"I don't understand. How is she solely responsible for that many deaths?" Riordan looked down at Storm as he continued. "I know that she was in the services and all, but that is a lot of kills for any one person."

"She didn't actually do any of the killing. But she did guide our missiles to a place where there were…this is difficult without involving you in things that you're not supposed to know." He got up to pace. "When she was recruited, it was figured out right away that she was special. Not just as a human, because we knew that was what she was, but her intelligence, as well as her innate ability to see things that none of us could. Like, she could see an outcome of a mission, see how people would react, how they would move when shit hit the fan. That day she was hit, she could see what no one, not even our boots on the ground, could see. Not just what was in her head, but she could see directly into the compound where we'd been told nothing was going on."

"It was a trap." Blackson nodded at his dad. "And the men, her men that were with her, were going in too. They were going to be killed right along with her but for the accident."

"It wasn't an accident. She and her men were targeted." He rubbed his hand over his face as he continued. "She knew before we sent them in. Told everyone that would listen that it was too easy, too quiet. But we knew better, or so we thought. Satellite had showed them that there were no forces in camp. The small compound had been abandoned. We were so wrong."

"That's enough." They all stared at Storm when she woke up. "I think you've bored these people long enough, Tony. And you've overstayed your welcome." He nodded, then reached into the back of his jacket and laid a gun on the tray in front of her. Then three clips.

Without a word to her, Blackson left. Storm picked up the gun, slammed a clip in the bottom of it, then racked the slide. She was as ready as she'd ever be if someone came in again. When she laid back on the bed, Riordan realized what that had cost her. She was still drugged up, but he'd bet any amount of money that if someone came in with ill intent, they were dead.

"Well, I don't know about anyone else, but I'm starved." His mom leaned into Storm and kissed her on the cheek before doing the same to him. "I love you. And remember what I told you, son." He nodded. His dad hugged him as well, then kissed Storm. They were gone in a few minutes. He looked at Storm.

"Are you leaving?" He shook his head and got one of the chairs and brought it closer to the bed. "Okay, let me rephrase that…when are you leaving?"

"I'm not until you're released. And they're saying tomorrow morning. While they know what she was giving you, they're not sure where she might have gotten it. Street form of heroin, and pure. But they're narrowing it down." He watched her face. Riordan noticed that she was tired, and he assumed it was from the drug. "Mom said that you were trying to get rid of her before this happened."

"Yeah. It works on her about like it does on you." He didn't say anything but smiled at her. "Why are you here? There is no reason for it."

"I'm beginning to think I made a major mistake with you." Yawning hugely, all Storm did was nod at him. "You're not at all what I thought you would be when I found my mate, but you're sort of growing on me."

"Yeah, like a fungus. Also, you should know that I'm mean. In the event you didn't notice that." She opened her eyes and looked at him. "But seriously, why are you still here? Don't you have some kind of job or something?"

"I do. And as of right now, I'm doing it." She asked him what he meant. "I want to get to know you, Storm. I think the only way that we're going to be able to make this work is if we try…if I try to be less of an asshole."

"Nah, I think that's too ingrained into your head for that to ever change." It took him a moment to realize she'd made a joke about him. At least he hoped it was a joke. "I'm not the kind of girl that men like you want to marry. I'm more the kind of girl that the guy takes out drinking because she knows the best bars and she can hold her liquor better than him. Also, men like you marry debs. I'm not a deb. I'm the one that protects the stupid deb."

"No, you're never going to be mistaken for a debutant. And I can picture you being the one that teaches our children how to protect themselves, shoot better than anyone else, and to be able to give other parents gray hairs." She was falling asleep, but he had no doubt that she was just as alert as if she were fully awake. "Would you like to have children with me, Storm?"

"No. You're too stiff and straight-laced. Do you even own a pair of jeans and a sloppy sweatshirt?" He told her that he didn't, but he was going to take care of that. "You'll probably want them ironed, too. Or buy some that already have tears in them, to make them look stressed or whatever. My pants are worn with pride. And they probably cost a quarter of what you'll pay for a pair that are already worn out. You're such a dweeb."

As she drifted more, he thought of the flowers that he'd had when he shifted. The roses that he now realized would have been a mistake. And chocolate. Getting chocolate, or for that matter any kind of sweets, for a person who baked like she did would be wrong as well. He thought of what she might like and had to laugh to himself. She would take a gun and ammo over flowers and candy any day, he'd bet. Riordan reached out for his brother Mac, the one who knew just what to get a girl.

*Her? Shit, Riordan, I don't have a clue. She's not like most women, and I think you know that.* He told her that he did. *Why don't you try taking her out? I mean, not to a romantic dinner, but a bar. Maybe one that has line dancing. Wait, no, that wouldn't work. She'd shoot you if you even suggested that.*

*Mom said I need to grovel. I'm not sure how to do that and not fall back into my usual mode of working around a woman.* Mac laughed. *I was thinking of doing something to me. Not leaving her, as she has told me to do numerous times, but she mentioned jeans and a sloppy sweat shirt.*

*Yeah, with her, casual is best. That way when she kicks your ass again, you won't ruin another suit. I heard that the other one you had on was beyond help. Come by the house when you leave there. I think I can help you out with that. Oh, and bring her along, too. There is something that I'd like to ask her. It's personal, not business. Tony said that she's got an instinct about things. I'd like to ask her advice on a place I'm thinking of buying.*

Riordan said that he would. When the door opened a few minutes later, Storm woke with her gun pointed at the door. The nurse stood there for several seconds before she reached slowly for her badge. She was military if he was looking at her badge correctly. But Storm obviously didn't trust that either. The gun never wavered at all.

"Who's your CO?" She told her it was Blackson. "Is he here still? If so, go and get him. I want to talk to him anyway."

When the door shut and opened again, Storm sat up in bed when the man himself entered. Blackson looked like he was going to hurt something as he tried his best not to laugh. The man had to try twice before he could speak.

"You scared ten years off that kid. I swear to you, she's going to think twice before working for me again." His laughter broke through then, and he just shook his head. "She was coming in to tell you that you can go when you're ready. I'm having you escorted and watched, but you can go. We won't have a run down on that shit for a couple more days.

Might as well let you go home and see what kind of trouble you can get in there."

"Clothes?" she asked him. Blackson nodded and tossed Riordan a duffle bag that felt too heavy when he caught it. "I'm not going to need protection. Save it for someone who does."

"Too bad. My boss said you do, and he's got a bit more pull than you do." He started out the door, then came back in. "Stormy, I'm sorry about this."

Storm nodded and reached for the bag. Blackson said he'd be in touch and left them alone. Riordan stood up to help her when she moved the blanket out of the way. The little nurse came back in just as he was trying to figure out how to work around the IV. He wasn't sure, but he thought that Storm was ready to pull it out on her own. The nurse had it out and a Band Aid—one with little happy faces on it—on her arm before either of them could say anything. Then she left them without a word.

Getting her to the side of the bed, Riordan got a good look at her legs. Lifting the sheet up higher on her thighs, he was surprised when she didn't stop him. The more he saw, the more he realized how lucky she really had been.

"The fire got me here. I was pretty close when they bombed the compound. I knew it was going to happen to me, but figured, like Blackson did, that it would incinerate me. I wasn't so lucky, I guess." He nodded and touched his fingers gently over the scars. "They tried skin grafts at first, but it was too extensive and there was too much damage done to them for it to work. Both my legs were broken, as well as the ankle on my left foot. It's what hurts me the most when I have been sitting for a while and have to get up. My legs, I mean."

He picked up her foot and turned it in his hands. She still hadn't stopped him, and he decided that he was going to look until she did. Lifting her foot to his mouth, he kissed the worst of the scars and then laid her leg back on the bed.

"Let me see all of you." Her head was shaking even before he finished speaking. But when he pushed her back on the bed, she let him. When he reached for the snaps on her gown, Storm turned to look away from him.

The sound of the snaps was loud in the quiet room. He pulled them free completely, on the left then right, before pulling the gown down from her neck. Her breasts were the first thing he saw—full and with dark pink nipples—before he saw the scars.

"We were driving to the compound when I saw the tree. There aren't that many in the area where we'd been fighting, and it sort of stuck out like a blister on your thumb. Most of them had been burned down for one reason or another. But that one was there...bare of leaves, but standing tall in an otherwise desolate area." The scar below her breast was about eight inches long and at least two inches wide. There were others, too, some small, some long and narrow, but he could see that the one that Blackson had told him about had caused her the most pain and suffering. "When the bomb went off under us, I knew we were all dead. I felt myself blast away. Then nothing. Brewer was driving and he just sort of exploded before I was thrown away. I didn't know anything for a while."

Riordan touched the scar, and ran his fingers down the length of it as she lay there. When her breath caught, he looked up at her. She was looking at him then, and he could see something there that he'd never seen on her face before.

"You were scared." Nodding, he touched his fingers to her breast, filled his hand with it as her nipple puckered under his touch. "I love the feel of your skin. It's soft and warm. I'd very much like to take a taste of your nipple, Storm."

"I'm not pretty like the women you know." He leaned down and took the pert flesh into his mouth. Nibbling gently on her, he closed his eyes when her hand curled into his hair. "Riordan, you'll regret this."

He lifted his head and looked at her. "No. I don't think I will. But I do need to see the rest of you. Know what those monsters did to you before you took them out."

Riordan helped her sit up, then to stand. She was unsteady now. Her legs, she told him, cramped up when she was off them for a while. As her strength came to her, he pulled her gown off her the rest of the way and turned her toward the bed. This was where most of the damage had been done to her. He could see that now.

"I landed in a tree. My tree. High up where no one could see me, I suppose, because who would have thought that I'd land there? I still had my headset on, and it worked. More than likely because of where I was more than there being no damage done to the radio in the truck. When I woke up, it was buzzing in my ear and it took me a few minutes to figure out it wasn't my head, but the people on the other end trying to find out what had happened." The scar here was wider, longer. It went from the top of her panties that she still wore to just beneath her scapula. Like on her belly, he touched his fingers to this one as well. And then the fifty or so others that were still pink in their newness. "The tree branch went through me. I could see it coming out of my chest and wondered for a long time after why it hadn't hit my kidneys. It had damaged the lower lobe of my lung, but I could still breathe, just not well."

Bending her at the waist, he pressed her head to the bed. He wanted her. Badly. His cock was aching so badly now that he had to cup himself or cause some serious harm. She was aroused, too. He thought that was why she was talking, trying to ignore how wet she was. Riordan ran his hands up her sides to her shoulders, then back down again, his thumbs pressing gently into her spine.

"Riordan. Please stop. I'm not...you're not supposed to want me." He rocked into her ass. She fit him well, and he put his hands on her hips and held her while he took his time fucking her this way. When she pressed back against him, making him ache more, he cupped her pussy from beneath and felt how wet she was. "Please."

"Come for me, love." Her head shook, but he pressed his fingers into her heat, the silky barrier making him want to rip them from her. "I want to drink from you, taste you when you come. But I need to feel you come in my hand. Come for me, Storm. Please."

Her breaths became pants; her body rode his hand. Even as she took her pleasure, he knew that if he wanted he could slide into her, fill her with his cum, and make her his. But her pleasure was first. Having her release like this was going to make her blood taste better.

"Riordan, please." He pulled his pants down, his cock stretching from his groin painfully. Sliding between her legs, he felt her soak him. His cock touched her clit, and she cried out. "Now. Fill me now, damn it."

He wanted to be gentle, but she wasn't having it. Riordan tried to bring her, just let his cock ride between her legs until she came, but she cried out again for him to take her, and Riordan felt her touch her fingers to his crown. It was all it took. Pulling back, he slid into her, her juices making the slide easy. She was so hot, so tight that he had to still or come before she did.

"Christ. Yes." His fingers were biting into her flesh. He knew that he'd leave a mark. When she moved back against him, he pushed forward. Leaning over her, cupping her pussy with one hand, her breast with the other, he fucked her as gently as he could. He didn't want to hurt her.

"Come with me."

He growled low when she commanded him. His cat was snarling at him to fill her, to mark her, but Riordan wanted this to last. Again, she wasn't letting him. And when she cried out she was coming, it was as if she pulled him with her. His entire body turned inside out, and he bit down on her shoulder as she screamed out her second release.

He held her to him. Riordan knew that he was too heavy. His body was pressing hers down onto the bed. But he felt good. Even his cat was purring along his flesh. When he stood up, bringing her with him, he held her until she stopped trembling. He knew that he'd hurt her when tears fell on his arm below her breasts. Holding her was all he could think to do. He'd hurt her again. Yes, it had been fantastic for the both of them, but he had hurt her badly. Riordan helped her to the bathroom then and turned on the shower while she held onto the counter. He was taking off his own clothing when she looked at him in the mirror.

"You can't take a shower with me." He stripped off his shirt, then his pants. "Really, you have to leave me alone now. You can't want to…you surely can't want to—"

"Oh, I want to. Again and again. But I think we should take it easy for a while. You've worn me down." He picked up the little things that had been left in the room for her…the smallest bottle of shampoo and body wash he'd ever seen, along with a toothbrush and paste. There was a comb, too, that was so cheap that when he picked it up to study it, three of the teeth broke off. "When we get to my apartment, we'll take a proper shower. I have all kinds of soaps, but you should have some there, too. Not that I mind you smelling like me, but—"

"Have you seen me?" He nodded and pulled her body to his. Riordan looked at the two of them in the mirror over the sink, but Storm was looking away. "I don't want to see me. And I can't believe you want to either."

"I think that what was done to you was horrific. But you survived, thankfully. You have some scarring that is terrible to look at, but again, you survived." He pulled her chin around so that she could see him in the mirror. "I think you're the most beautiful creature I've ever seen. And those marks on your body are what makes you what you are."

"You mean a bitch." He laughed and told her no. Then he kissed her on the mouth and helped her use the toothbrush. Her hands were stiff, too, and he worried for her.

He helped her into the shower, not even sure what to say to her about not looking. He loved her body, scars and all. But he didn't think she'd believe him if he told her. Storm did allow him to wash her back, and she washed his, too. His cock was full and aching again when they got out, and she kept telling him they were done, there would be no more sexual contact between them. He didn't even bother pointing out her flushed skin, hard nipples, and the scent of her need making his cat want her, too.

As soon as she was dressed again—the clothing in the duffle had been for them both—he pulled her body to his and kissed her. She held onto him until he lifted his head and looked down at her.

"We're going to talk, you and I." Shaking her head, she told him that he was insane. "Perhaps, but I'm also not sure what you thought I'd do once I saw your body. Or have you had this come up before?"

When she looked away, he knew. Someone had done this to her. And when he found them, because he would, Riordan was going to rip them apart and see how well they liked looking in the mirror.

# CHAPTER 6

They'd had sex. Really good sex, too, and now he wasn't running from her. As he drove them to her house, she tried to think what had gone wrong. Maybe it was a pity fuck. That's what Mark had called it when she'd—

"When I bit you, we formed a link that makes it so we can read each other's mind. Did you know that?" Her face heated up when she thought of all the things that had been going on in her head. "Yeah. Anyway, it wasn't a pity fuck. And when I find this Mark person, I'm going to show him the errors of his ways."

"Why?" He asked her what she meant. "Why do you care? I mean, I'm not sure why you didn't run for the hills either, but you don't have to be all macho now that you think you owe me something. I'm quite capable of taking care of my own sex life if I want."

The truck took a hard turn, and she held on when he glanced at her. "You use a vibrator? Can I watch you while you come? Christ, I was hard before, but now I'm about to break, I'm hurting so much."

She looked at his cock and could see the outline of it in his pants. He was hard, thick too. And when he'd filled her, she'd thought that no one had ever felt that good. When his hand cupped his cock and he said her name, she looked up at his face.

"I would like nothing more than to pull over, slide over on the seat, and take you right here. To have you riding me while I suckle at your breasts, have you holding me while you come." He moaned, and she felt her own body react to him. "Storm, if I pull over right now, will you let me taste you?"

"We're on the highway." He nodded and moaned again. "Stop that. You can't be horny again, you just came. Men don't come…what are you doing?"

He was pulling off the highway and onto a residential street. As he drove into a parking lot, way out from the other cars, Storm felt her pussy swell and get hot. As soon as he turned off the engine and reached for her, she moved toward him. Christ, she was going to be hard pressed to run this guy off.

"I'm not going anywhere."

He took her mouth before she could answer him. She had no idea what she might have said to him, but his hands were stripping her of her shirt even as she sat over his lap. As she was braless now, he took her entire breast into his mouth as she wrapped her hand around his now bare cock.

He lifted her up enough to pull her pants off. The sound of them tearing, the feel of them being torn from her body, had her panting. Her need was so spiked that she wasn't sure if she could wait to have him inside of her. But as soon as he pulled her down, impaling her over him, she cried out her climax as he bit into her breast.

"Ride me, Storm. I want to feel you riding me." She'd never done this before so she had to have help. He was sucking so hard at her breasts—first one then the other—that she couldn't think beyond coming—and soon. When he pulled her closer to him, bringing her clit right up against his body when he did, she came again, screaming out his name as he pulled her head to his shoulder. "Bite me. Sink your teeth into me, love, and mark me as yours."

She had no choice in the matter. It was as if her entire existence had been for this moment, the moment that she was going to bite someone. *Bite Riordan Harrison* looped in her head over and over until she had to do it. When she licked the pounding pulse, felt the heat of it under her tongue, he cried out and told her *now*. Biting into him came as natural to her as breathing, and the taste of his blood brought her twice more as it filled her mouth and she swallowed it down.

Darkness seemed to come in waves. Stars sparkled behind her eyelids as she swallowed again. When he bit into her shoulder, Storm cried out against his throat. Pulling away from him, she threw back her head and let the climax of all climaxes take her. This time the darkness pulled her under completely, and she simply let it.

When she opened her eyes, she was still on his lap. Riordan was talking to someone and she wasn't sure if they'd been caught or he was on the phone. He lifted her head up and winked at her, and she saw the phone and started to move off his lap. He held her to him as he spoke in the phone.

"I'm not sure what to tell you, Isabell. But I've made it clear from the beginning that I'm not into having a long-term relationship with you. It was a mutual benefit for us both. And now, it's at an end." This time she tried harder and he let her. But when she tried to scoot away from him, he picked her up and put her on his lap. "No, I told you, I don't want to see you once more. I'm seeing someone else now and it's very serious." Storm could hear the woman on the other end now.

"Well, I don't know why you think this is going to be any longer lasting than any other relationship you've had. You do know that you're not capable of loving someone other than yourself, don't you?" She sounded snarky, and Storm took an immediate dislike to her. "Besides, you know that in a few weeks you'll come running back to me. We're really good in bed, and when this is over, I might take you back. Oh, forget that. Marry the girl and we can just fuck on the side. What do you say? The little woman doesn't have to know about it."

"I'll know." He looked down at Storm as he continued talking to Isabell. "And this isn't a relationship. This is the real deal. I've fallen in love with her and I'm going to try my best to convince her to marry me. Soon."

The laughter at the other end had Storm wanting to find the bitch and punch her in her no doubt pretty face. When Riordan laughed, she glared at him and he cut the call off, telling Isabell he had to go.

"You should call her back and tell her you've changed your mind." He asked her why he'd do that. "Because while I have no idea what she looks like, I'm betting that she's much prettier than I'll ever be and has a body to die for."

"Yours is better." He laughed when she snorted at him. "It is. Your breasts are full and I simply love your nipples. The way that they swell up and tighten in my mouth. The way you take me, and your pussy wraps around my cock like it's a nice warm glove. And when you come, you scream out my name so prettily that I want to make you come over and over again."

"Stop that." He handed her the shirt she'd had on before he'd pulled over. "This is just stupid, you know. We could have been caught. Then what would you have said to your family?"

"I'm sure that they will be thrilled to death that I've finally taken a mate. And I know that my mom is going to be bugging you soon about grandchildren. She's always had her heart set on granddaughters. I'm thinking it has to do with having six sons. But I bet she'd be happy with just a grandchild—"

"You can't be serious." He told her that he was. "I don't understand you. Even before we had sex, I never understood you. I think I liked you better when you...when we.... I just liked you better before."

As he pulled his pants up over his body, he said nothing. She was sure that she'd pissed him off, and for some reason that hurt her, too. Not that she hadn't given him good reason to be mad, but she was hurt by that all the same.

"My mom wants us to come over for dinner. Is that all right with you?" Storm nodded. "And I guess your aunts are invited, too. My dad already picked them up and has them at the house. Also, she said that there are three men waiting for you. She's not sure what they're doing there, but they're dressed in fatigues and armed."

"My guards." He nodded and started the truck. She was still pulling on her pants when he pulled her to him again. This time he looked deep into her eyes rather than kissing her like she had expected him to do. "I don't know what to do. I'm better at orders, and timelines. I can order around a platoon of men and have them working in short order. But you and this, whatever this is, it scares me more than being on the front line."

"I'm scared, too." He kissed her then and got back under the wheel. "I'm going to tell you something that you might not know. I'm very possessive of you. And when my brothers touch you, rub their faces against yours, I'm going to take you back to my place and fuck you like you've never been fucked before."

"I don't think I can survive you and sex." He laughed and drove them back to his parents' house. She had a feeling that things with this man would never be easy or go gently in the night.

~~~

Isabell turned first right, then left, looking at her reflection in the mirror. There was no way that she was going to give up this easy, and there wasn't any way that she was going to give up on Riordan. He was the perfect man for her no matter how many other women he took to his bed. She might not even care so long as he satisfied her just as much as he did this other woman. Whoever she was. And as for him marrying this other woman, that wasn't going to happen either. She had her sights on him, and everyone else was going to have to go to hell.

"You don't even love him. And I'm sure that he's not in love with you. Why are you doing this to yourself?" Her mother was sitting on her bed amongst the discarded clothing that she'd tried on and dismissed after hanging up on Riordan. She refused to think that he'd hung up on her. Isabell turned to her and picked up the shoes she had decided went well with this dress. "Isabell, he said he's found someone else. You should just let him go. You can't be seriously thinking that he's going to drop her after you said he confessed to loving this other woman. It's just not right."

"I will not let him go. He's mine. And if I can't have him, I have no intentions of sharing him with some upstart that thinks she can have him, too." Her mother asked her what she intended to do. "I'm not sure yet, but he's not going to know what hit him when he sees me at his mom's house. I should have been there long before now. And this dress will make him realize what it is he's giving up for her."

"You mean to just go there unannounced?" Isabell nodded as she pulled her shoes on. "That is not the way things are done. You know that. What if this girl is there? What if she's more than you expect?"

"Never. We've been dating for almost two years now, and he's mine." Riordan was the type of man who made woman look at her with envy. Men, too, for that matter. And when she entered a room with him right at her side, people knew that this was the kind of couple they wanted at their homes and parties. "I know that he told me from the start that there would never be anything more between us than dating and sex, but I'm not going to give up. This is just a small fling for him. He's gotten cold feet about us and he's backing off. I'm just going to show him that he doesn't have to."

"What you're going to show him is that you're a desperate woman who doesn't know when to stop." Isabell glared at her mother. "When you get this thrown back in your face, I'm going to be here to say I told you so. I tried to tell you from the very beginning that Riordan wasn't a man to trifle with. And I was right. He's going to hurt you and us too, if you pursue this."

"I don't know what you're talking about. He's not even in the same league as us." Her family was old money, and while they didn't have nearly the amount that the Harrisons did, they did have the added prestige of being the Applegates of Hyde Park. Her family had been one of the first to build a mansion in that area, and the estate was still there. "He has money, yes, and a great deal of it, but we know how to spend it."

She thought her mother said something like "You do," but she was going out the door. Riordan would marry her. They'd have two beautiful children that a nanny would care for, and the two of them would go on fabulous vacations where they'd have their pictures taken for all those magazines that followed movie stars around.

Isabell knew that she was vain and spoiled. Her daddy had said that little girls were meant to be treated like queens and pampered by the best. When he'd died three years ago, she'd felt as if she'd had her heart ripped from her chest. Her mother had never treated her the way he had. Her voice was that of reason, her dad had told her, and that on occasion, she should listen to her. But Mother had never given her everything she wanted, and not once had she called her princess, like Daddy had.

The limo driver held the door open for her, and she slipped inside. As soon as the door closed behind her, she leaned back, but not too far so as not to muss her hair. Riordan was going to be so happy to see her, Isabell knew it. Fussing with her dress, she made sure that it looked just right so that he could see her long legs when she was helped out of the car. Isabell thought of all the ways he was going to beg her to take him back. And he would, too.

The ride took longer than she thought it should. And when she asked the driver where they were, he told her that they were in the country, whatever that meant. But when they stopped twenty minutes later, she had a feeling that they were lost, and he had to ask for directions. As far as Isabell was concerned, he'd lost his job as of the moment they got back to her home. But he opened the door for her, and she had no choice but to get out. If this was a joke, she didn't think it was funny.

The house was nice. It was larger than her home, and the pillars out front were made of stone, not wood as the ones at their house were. She was wondering if they could have their home look just like this one when a tall handsome man came out of the house. Isabell fluffed her hair and put on her best smile. Whoever this was, she wouldn't mind having a bite or two of him.

"Are you lost?" She told him she had no idea and tried her best lost look on him. "Yeah, we don't get a lot of your kind coming out here in the evening. At least—"

"What do you mean, my kind?" He laughed, and she felt her temper rise. "I'm looking for the Harrison family. Perhaps you can direct my driver to the correct address and we can be on our way."

"You're here." She looked around again and thought this had to be a lie. "My parents live here, and have since they got married. My brothers and I have for the most part moved out, but we're all here now."

"I'm looking for Riordan. He's my…we're dating." He looked at her oddly with a cocked brow that made her want to try it, too. She so envied people who had talent like that. Then she realized that he was speaking. Her asking him to repeat himself had him laughing again.

"I said, Riordan is here, too, with Stormy. She's in the back with a couple of men, and Dad and another guest are in the office with Riordan." Isabell asked him who Stormy was, his sister? "No, she's Riordan's fiancée. I guess she'll be my sister when they marry, but for now, she's just a good friend. Were you invited here today?"

He knew that she'd not been invited and she wanted to smack that knowing grin off his face. When he turned and started up the steps again, Isabell had no choice but to follow. This was not going the way she'd hoped. And when she entered the house, she knew how wrong she'd been about Riordan and his money. She'd bet anything that his money was older than hers.

The house was massive. The entryway alone was bigger than her room. And the marble floors and beautiful Chippendale table in the center of it shone to a brilliant shine. The vase was more than likely as old as the house, and the flowers in it were bright and colorful, nothing like she'd ever seen before. Beyond the hallway was a staircase that was at least ten feet wide and split at the large stained glass mural at the top. She was just dying to see what beauty was up there as well. This was a house that Isabell would love to live in forever.

When she saw who she assumed was Riordan's mother, Isabell thought maybe she should have taken her mom's advice and stayed home. This woman didn't look like she'd be a pushover as she had hoped she'd be. The look on her face told her that she had interrupted something, and she wasn't at all happy with her for doing so. It wasn't a good way to start what Isabell hoped would be a long and wonderful relationship.

"Hello, Mrs. Harrison. I was hoping to find Riordan. I don't know why, but I thought my driver was taking me to his house, not here." The man that had met her in the yard laughed. She glared at him as she put out her hand for Mrs. Harrison. "There must have been some sort of mess up."

"I'm sure." The woman took her hand, and Isabell thought she was trying to crush it. As she pulled it back, Mrs. Harrison smiled at her, as if she knew just what she'd done. "Riordan is talking to his dad and one of the partners. There were some issues at the office today, and they're trying to work it out. But Stormy is here. I think whatever she was doing with her men is taken care of. I'll just call for her. I'm sure she'd love to meet you."

Before she could tell her that was all right, Stormy was called for. Isabell watched the woman coming toward her and rethought everything that had been going through her head. This was the woman he'd given her up for? Christ, she could barely walk. And she was dressed in what appeared to be scrubs, of all things. When she put out her hand to shake it, she had a moment of panic. The other woman just stared at it as if she had some sort of dirt on her.

"You must be the ex-girlfriend. You're just what I expected." Isabell had no idea how to take that so said nothing. "You're kind of...I don't know...girly, aren't you?"

"I'm a woman. What are you?" The woman laughed, and it sounded like she really was enjoying this. "You should really work on your manners some. Riordan expects his dates to be delicate and well behaved. And well dressed. What are you wearing?"

"Well, then he's shit out of luck since he started seeing me." The woman moved around her, like she was inspecting her or something. And Isabell thought she found her lacking in every way. "You're not in very good shape, are you? Kind of flabby. You should really try to join a gym or something. Might take away some of the cellulite you have under that dress of yours."

"What?" Isabell looked around for someone to help her. Mrs. Harrison was there, but she wasn't going to be any help. The woman could barely stand she was laughing so hard. And the young man that had met her at the car was sitting on the steps laughing as well. She looked at the woman again. "Just who the hell to you think you are talking to me this way? I'll have you know that I come from a good family with the proper upbringing. I'm not flabby, nor do I have cellulite, as you have suggested. Why am I even bothering with you? Surely Riordan knows that you're no match for me."

"I'm Storm Browning. I do have a pedigree like you think you have, but that doesn't really matter much to me. Dogs make me itch." Isabell was sure she'd been insulted again but wasn't sure. Storm continued on with her introduction, if that was what it was. "My family has more money and more prestige than you do in all of your entire linage. Not that it means all that much to me, but it's there should I ever want to claim it. How about you, Isabell Applegate? How much is enough for you? Or do you think there is no limit to the amount you could get your hands on?"

"Money? You? I doubt that very much. Just look at you. I'm here to see Riordan. I don't have any idea what you think you're trying to prove with me, but it won't work." Storm just smiled and nodded. "You're just a fling with him. Nothing more than a good lay and something to keep me in line."

"It's a good fuck, honey, not lay, and he is good at that." Isabell felt her face heat up. "You really should get that stick out of your ass and maybe someone might show you the difference sometime. I can tell you about it if you really want to know."

"I most certainly do not."

Isabell was ready to call for Riordan when she saw him. She had no idea how long he'd been standing there, but she thought it rude that he'd not come to her rescue sooner. As he straightened up from the newel post that he'd been leaning on, she put out her hand for him to take it. There was no way this woman was real. It had to be a joke that he'd given her up for this thing. But he moved by her and put his arm around the woman.

"Isabell, I didn't know you were coming here." She didn't know how to respond to him. There was so much anger in his voice that she thought for sure he was upset with Storm for speaking to her this way. "I see you've met my Stormy. She's a little on the blunt side. You'll have to forgive her."

"No, I don't. She's rude and nasty. You shouldn't allow her to talk to me this way, Riordan. It's not the way I was raised. And I'm thinking it wasn't the way you were raised either." She looked at him then and let the tear she'd not had to manufacture fall down her cheek. "I want you to tell me this is a joke. I don't know how long it will take me to forgive you for this, but you know how I dislike these kinds of situations."

"He doesn't allow or disallow me to do anything. I make my own decisions." Storm looked ready to pounce on her when she heard something or someone coming from the back of the house. The noise that came from behind Riordan had her looking that way. And when the man came into the room more, she thought for sure she was seeing things.

"President Waynewright. I had no idea that you knew the Harrison family." He just smiled at her and put out his hand. She shook it, thinking that this alone should make Riordan see what a real woman acted like.

"I don't know them. Well, I didn't know them. I came to talk to my girl, Stormy. She's been helping me out with a little problem I was having."

Isabell thought she'd heard him wrong. But when he pulled the woman to him and kissed her on the head, Isabell felt like she'd been punked. Then she realized that was what was really going on.

"I get it now. I see. I'm not one for a good joke. My Riordan can tell you that. But this is a good one. I nearly fell for it." Isabell put her hand out to the president again. "I don't think we've been properly introduced. I'm Riordan's fiancée, Isabell Applegate. The Applegates of Hyde Park. Perhaps you know of my family?"

"I can't say that I do." President Waynewright looked at Riordan, then at Stormy. "I thought you said he was going to marry you? Not that I care. I'd been hoping all this time you'd tell me I was the light of your life."

The low growl coming from Riordan had her taking a step back. But then everyone laughed and she tried to join them. Isabell was so confused that she was willing to turn to Stormy for help.

"You're not going to marry him, are you? Tell me you're just kidding me and I'll completely understand." Storm just stared at her, and Isabell wanted to cry. "You're not his type. I mean, you don't even look like you have ten cents in your pocket, and just look how you're dressed. Those are not designer pants. They look like…they look military."

"Because they are." Storm reached behind her and pulled out a wallet. An actual wallet that looked like something a man would carry. "These are my credentials. I'm dressed this way because I am military. Not that I have to answer any of your questions, but no, I'm not marrying Riordan, but only because he's never asked. I might live with him. As you've pointed out, he is a good fuck. As for marrying him, I don't know. But you'll be the first to know when I come to a decision."

Isabell wasn't going to stand here and take this abuse. If he wanted someone with a temper, who spoke her mind, she knew that she could do that, too. Her maid was forever telling her she talked like a man. And if one of them could see her when she was locked up in her room, they'd run from her.

"I don't care for the way you're speaking to me." She looked at Riordan. "You should take better care of your…pets, Riordan. And the next time I see you, you'd better be dressed properly. I won't stand for this…whatever it is you're wearing. I expect you to be well groomed and attentive. You have been remiss in that so far today."

Someone laughed, and she turned to him. The older man looked like he might be related to the rest of them, but right now, she was showing herself to be strong. Taking a step to him, she slapped him across the face.

Isabell felt her arm being jerked behind her, and the hard point of something at her head. She tried to jerk from it when Storm—she just realized who it was—told her not to fucking move. That was when she realized it wasn't her finger at her head but a gun. Isabell tried again to break free when her arm suddenly popped.

The pain of it was incredible, but no matter how much she screamed to be let go, Storm held her. Looking at the men in front of her, she thought for sure one of them would help her, Riordan at the very least, but they were stepping back, as if they were afraid of her, too.

"She's hurting me." Mrs. Harrison stepped in front of her, and Isabell smiled as best she could through the pain. "Could you please tell her to unhand me? She's hurting me."

"Yes, and you're very lucky that it's her holding you and not me. If you ever draw back and hit one of my family again, especially my husband and mate, I will tear you apart. And I do mean literally tear you into tiny little pieces that will never be found. Then I will urinate on your remains. Do you understand me?" Isabell knew a kind of fear that had never been in her life before. The gun at her head was nothing compared to the terror that she was feeling from the woman standing in front of her. "Now then, Stormy is going to let you go, gently. Then you're going to get out of my house and never return. If I so much as hear of you talking badly about my son and his fiancée, I will do as I have said. And in case you're not understanding me, this is not a threat, young lady, but a promise I make to you with all sincerity."

Storm took her to the door. The gun was removed finally, but she held her arm up behind her like she was going to tear it off. As soon as they were out of the house, her driver opened the door for her, but never came to her rescue. When she felt Storm near her ear, Isabel whimpered.

"You come back here and what Bri will do to you will be a walk in the park compared to what I will do to you if I get to you first. Stay away from my family. Do you understand me?" She nodded. "Good. And when you get home, I would not call the papers and tell them what happened here today; I wouldn't tell my buddies…all wimpy, cellulite-assed fucking bitches like you, I'm sure. If one word of this gets around, if a single word is printed in the papers, you'll wish you'd never met me."

"I already wish that." She stumbled forward when Storm pushed her away. As she made her way to the limo, she tried to control her terror. There was something very wrong with these people, Isabell concluded. And as she got into the car, she looked up at her driver. It was on the tip of her tongue to tell him to take her to the police station, or at the very least to the hospital, when he looked at her. His grin had her thinking that he knew just what had happened in the house.

"You're fired." He laughed and shut the door on her. As the car started up and she was tossed around in the back, she thought she should have waited until they got home to fire him. The ride was not going to be a pleasant one.

# CHAPTER 7

Ordan entered the bakery at ten the next morning. He was there for two reasons, and he was as excited with one as he was with the other. An assignment, his missus told him, and only he could do it. He so loved his wife that he thought he'd get her some flowers on the way home. Then he remembered that it was Wednesday and the maid's day off, and he thought of getting her two dozen. Then see if he could persuade her to run in the woods with him. Yes, it was going to be a good day all around.

Lynn handed him a Danish on his way by her. Sally gave him a cup of coffee and he thought if he came here very often, he'd have to get out more for exercise. Ordan thought he'd already put on a few pounds since meeting the young girl who had taken his heart. When he entered the back room, he was surprised to see his son there, apparently icing cookies. And he appeared to be doing a crappy job of it, too.

"Son?" Riordan growled at him, and Ordan had to sit down. He was going to end up getting himself hurt if he laughed right now. "Don't you have another job? I mean, at the office?"

"Christina ran me off. Said that I was useless to her. I have no idea what she was talking about, but the next thing I knew I had my briefcase and jacket and was in the elevator. And when I got here, Storm told me I was going to be useful or go home." He shoved the cookie he was mangling away from him and growled again. "This is stupid work."

"It is not stupid work. But you're doing a shitty job of it, and that's why you don't like it." Ordan watched Stormy pull a tray of cookies from the oven and put in another one as she continued berating Riordan. "If you took the time to listen to me, I would tell you how to ice them, but you have to be Mr. Know-it-all and learn on your own. Hello, Mr. Harrison. How are you today?"

"Fine. Call me Ordan, please." She didn't answer him, as she'd done the other times he'd asked her to call him that. "I've come here for some questions to be answered. Bri and I were at the table this morning, having some of those wonderful cheese things that you sent over, and we had a few come up. Questions I mean, not the Danish. I was wondering if I could maybe get them cleared up."

"Sure, but you're going to have to be prepared for me to answer them honestly. I'm not going to give you half-truths." He nodded, and expected some of the questions to have answers that would embarrass him. "Great. Let me get something to drink and take these up front. I'm having a productive day despite the interruptions."

Ordan looked at his son. He wondered if he knew that he was in love with her yet. The boy was nearly drooling to have her close to him. It was one of the things on his list today. A wedding date.

"She's feeling better." Ordan told Riordan that he could see that, but he wondered if either of them knew why. "When we get things settled here today, I'm going to go over with her and see her house. Danny is going to take over the upstairs. The rooms are too small for me and I can't really work up there either."

One more thing to wipe off the list...where they were going to live. "I was talking to Harold...to think we've had the president in our home, and he wants us to call him by his first name. Anyway, back to that. He said that she had a fine house, not far from where our home is. Imagine that."

"She said that it was her parents' house. I guess they died when she was little. Her grandmother raised her for a while, but Stormy was too much for her. The aunts took her rather than having her put in the system where she more than likely would have been hurt or worse, knowing her the way I do. I guess she was just as much a handful then as she is now." Ordan could see that she'd be too much for an elderly woman, and thought her aunts had done a bang-up job of making her a person of worth.

Stormy came back into the kitchen and looked into the five stacked ovens in the corner. Setting the timer, she sat down and smiled at him.

"Riordan telling you what a bitch I've been? I told him we could talk about marriage when I'm in the mood. Might not be for generations yet, but I'm not ready just yet. He might find he likes that Isabell person more."

Ordan hoped not and said so. "She's a terror. I never...she actually hit me. I wasn't even the one who laughed, Ennis did. And she hit me." He patted Stormy on the hand and winked at her. "But you and Bri protected me, didn't you, love?"

"Dad, stop flirting with my future wife. And for the record, we will not be waiting generations. I would very much like for you to take this seriously and say yes. I have asked you to marry me. Twice now, as a matter of fact." Stormy just rolled her eyes at Riordan, and he glared. "This is not up for discussion, Storm. I'm serious."

"Oh, speaking of serious, Mr. President called me this morning and reminded me about this thing he has going on at the White House. He wanted to extend an invitation to you and the rest of your family. I have to go, but you guys don't if you—"

"We're invited to the White House? Oh my, this is getting better and better all the time. We'd love to go. Are we to dress up and everything?" She told him it was black tie. "Yes, I'll have to dust off my old tux. I wonder if it still fits. And, of course, Bri will need to be all dolled up. This is exciting news. Thank you."

Stormy looked embarrassed, and he nearly asked her why she had to go. It didn't seem like it was her thing, dressing up for an outing. He wondered if she even owned a dress, much less high heels. But she cleared her throat, and he looked at her.

"You said you had some questions for us to answer?" Ordan nodded and thought of the list. He'd been here for less than an hour and the two of them had answered many of them already. But there were more.

"When I met you the first time, you knew what I was. I've been trying to think how you knew that not only was I a tiger, but that Mac and Riordan were my sons." She nodded and picked up one of the white iced cookies that were on the tray. "If you don't want to answer, I completely understand."

"No. It's not that. It's just…when I was with my men, we would talk about the strangest things. There were things that were off limits, of course, to most people. We never talked about the mission that we'd been on, who had not made it, nor did we talk about religion, politics, or race. Not that we didn't have a few crude jokes about all three, but we did try to keep it light." The cookie looked great when she set it down and picked up the next. He watched her face. This was a woman who rarely did anything without fully thinking it through. She and Riordan were very much alike in that. "What I'm going to tell you, very few people knew. Tony did, of course. He and I had the same kind of bond."

"He bit you." Stormy nodded at Riordan when he spoke. "That's how he knew that you were in trouble that day at the hospital. He had your blood."

"Yes. And the others in my group, too, that were paras. Actually, all nine of my men were. And when I say men, I mean both sexes. I had seven men and two women who worked with me. All of them wolf, believe it or not. I think Tony had a hand in that." Ordan thought he had, too, but said nothing. "When we sat around, either going from one point to another or on a plane to go somewhere that was not that easy to drive to, we'd talk about shit. Mostly what we were going to do when we got out. How we were going to go from killer to human again. And that was when they told me what they were."

Ordan thought that she was hurting from the memories and nearly told her to forget it. But Riordan touched his hand and when he looked at him, he shook his head. He supposed she did need to talk about things, but he didn't want her to hurt because of it. Ordan just hated to be the one to make her sad.

"We were more than just a team, a squad. I thought of us as a single unit, and we were. Communication was quiet and easy. They could see things better at night or in bad weather than I could using night goggles. And with this freaky thing I could do, you know, sort of see the conclusion to a mission before we did it, we were safe, kept each other safe." Ordan asked her if they ever shifted. "Yes. We had special packs full of clothing that one of us would be responsible for. One of them would go ahead of us, as a wolf, and lay them out, close to the place where we were headed. Then as one as their other selves, they'd go ahead of me, guiding me where to step, when to pause. There were times when one or more of them would cover me with their bodies as a troop would walk by us. It was what kept us alive as we were going in and out of dangerous situations."

She got up to check the ovens again, and Ordan noticed something he doubted even she had. Looking at Riordan, Ordan thought he didn't even see it. She was stronger. And not only that, she moved with more ease, too. Stormy was careful still, getting up slowly and moving with a slight limp, but he'd bet that in a few days she'd not even do that.

"What's your next question? I'm not sure...I think I answered that for you, didn't I?" He nodded. He picked up his list and she did another cookie. For every one of Riordan's messes, she did a dozen perfectly decorated ones.

"What are you? I mean, you're human, I know that, but what are you in the service?" He flushed slightly. "I'm sorry, I'm rude."

"No, you're not. I'm Special Forces." Danny snorted from across the room, and Ordan realized that the man had been listening to them. "I am Special Forces."

"Yeah, that's like saying that I'm a man. She's more than just the Special Forces. She *is* Special Forces." Ordan asked him what he meant. "Do you know what that means? The term Special Forces?"

"I know that they're highly trained men and women who can do some extraordinary things. That they're the ones that are called on to do what others can't." Danny nodded and told him that there was a lot more. "I'm sure that there is, but what does this have to do with her title?"

"She and her squad were Green Berets, army. And when you called in the Browning Squad, you could pretty much know that the shit had hit the fan and there ain't no hope for anyone else getting them out or getting the job done." Stormy told Danny he was exaggerating. "No, I'm not. I seen you in action, you know that. They could jump from a moving plane and land in water in a way that you'd never see a drop come back up and touch you. Shoot a rifle so good...hell, you couldn't even see the person firing the rifle, much less what he was aiming at, until the person at the receiving end was dead. 'Cause if they shot at you, you was dead. If you had to be brunged out cause you got your fool self caught behind enemy lines, you'd pray for them to be the ones that come for you. There just ain't none better than the Browning Squad."

Ordan looked at Stormy with new eyes. Here she sat, putting happy faces on cookies, and she had been in situations that no one might ever know about. She didn't acknowledge or deny Danny's comments. Ordan looked at Riordan and wondered just how much he'd known of what was said, and had a feeling that it was very little. As she sat there, Ordan wasn't sure what to do when she spoke again.

"That last day we were together was going to be nothing, they told us. Not that I believed it. But we were going to be ready no matter what. The powers that be said that there were no guns where we were headed. No artillery and certainly no ground warfare. It was going to be a search and rescue for anyone who had been left behind, and then we'd spend a few days just huddled up and resting. I had ordered a dozen steaks to be air dropped for us, and we were going to have a party." She set down the last of the cookies that they'd been working on and looked away. Ordan had a feeling she wasn't with them any longer.

~~~

Hanging from the tree, she knew that she was as good as dead. Below her she could see the enemy scrambling to get the ruined Humvee off the road and the bodies taken away. They would use this ploy again, she knew that, and the next time there would be more men and women killed. When the mike in her ear squawked, she thought it was the men below her, but then she heard a voice that sounded like heaven to her.

"Stormy, for Christ's sake, will you answer me?" She had sobbed just a little…the relief that she'd be able to talk to someone was profound. And Tony Blackson was the only person she knew who could help her right now. "Stormy?"

"They're dead." He told her of course they were, and for some reason that had struck her as funny even back then. "My men are all dead. I don't know what happened, but the rest of my team is gone. Three loaded and they're all gone."

Three loaded Humvees had been in line with her. The one she'd been in was in the middle and had sustained most of the damage, but the other two were just as badly twisted metal as the one she'd been in.

"We're coming for you." She told him no. She was as good as gone. "I can't leave you there. If they find you, they'll...I don't have to tell you what they'll do to you."

"I know, but they don't see me." She told him where she was. "Don't bother. I'm not going to make it no matter what you do to try and save me."

She must have fuzzed out because when she woke up, he was screaming in her ear. It was dusk now and the lights from the compound where they had been headed were bright enough that she could see a great deal more. Storm looked at where the wreckage had been. The Humvees were gone and so were her men. Storm looked down at her body. The branch was protruding from her chest by at least a foot, and it was slick with her blood. The knowledge of her impending death grew more certain with every breath, as the pain made her sick and dizzy.

"Storm, you have to help us. We need to know what you can see. Are more there? More men?" She started to tell him she had no idea, her body hurt too much to care right now, when he continued. "We need to take this guy out. He needs to be gotten rid of. Tell me what you can see, Stormy."

"They're underground. I can see them coming up from under some kind of underground shelter." Tony asked her if it was women and children. "No, not that I can see. They're armed, and with gear that looks new. Mostly rifles, but I can see handguns too. I can see four...no five tanks under some kind of tarps. And mortars. Several of them, lined up ready to load."

"They're getting ready for you." She told him that's what it looked like to her. "There's a convoy coming that way, about an hour from you. They'll be in the line of fire in less than that. I need to bring in an air strike. But I don't have anyone there on the ground. I need for you to guide them for me."

"All right. I can see their marks from here. I have the right equipment on me." She did too, a lot of it. Even a first aid kit that she couldn't get to in her pack. "I'm pretty close to the compound, but I don't think…."

"How close are you? I'm thinking you're going to be in the line of fire, aren't you? I really need to take this bastard out, Stormy, and you're the only one that can do it." She looked down at her body again. The blood was spilling onto the ground below her. The branch that she was literally hanging from was saturated with it, too. Shifting to another position caused her to cry out, and she heard him cursing. Then he spoke again. "Tell me how far you are from the place and if you can get away."

"I can't move. I'm going to die here soon, and there isn't shit you can do about it. I'm not going to be able to move even if I could. I told you, I'm stuck in this fucking tree. I can see it sticking from my chest, General. I'm not even sure how I'm still alive right now."

"Because you're a soldier and you know that you can't die until this thing is over." She told him yes, sir, and waited for him to tell her what was going to happen. "I have three coming in. Can you see them yet?" She could and told him so.

~~~

"Within four minutes the place was toast." She looked at the three men standing there and wondered what she'd said to them that had them looking so horrified. "I'm sorry. I did get off on a tangent, didn't I?"

"That's what happened to your legs. They hit you when they bombed the place." She nodded at Riordan. "How long before they came to get you?"

"Not long, less than forty-eight hours from the time I got there until they came to get me. I don't think they expected me to still be alive. Tony was certainly surprised, if I remember correctly. After that, I don't remember much else. Just his shocked look." Her aunt came in the back then, and her laughter broke the spell of the room. "What are you out of now?"

"The tables are here. The ones we got off that…. Is something wrong, love? Are these men…want me to poison their Danish? I can, you know."

Stormy kissed her cheek as she moved to the front of the bakery. The rest followed; the sounds of their chairs scraping made her aware of that.

Two trucks were in front of the shop, and the men standing there waiting for them looked like they could have lifted them without any problem. Not just the tables—and they looked heavy enough—but the whole fucking truck. Just as she was trying to figure out how many of the tables and chairs were theirs, a large SUV pulled up and four men and Mrs. Harrison spilled out of it.

"Just in time." She looked at Ordan, then at the men again as he continued. "You guys can help out and I'll buy you lunch. Stormy, I'd like for you to meet my sons, all of them, save Ennis. Where is he, anyway?"

"Doctoring. When I talked to him, he said he'd be along, but it would be a bit. Something about stitches and a kid that had less sense than he did muscles." Aedan winked at her. "Hello, love. Is Riordan treating you right? If not, let me know. I'll hurt him for you." Storm told him she was more than capable of doing that on her own.

The men, not boys, had been at the house the other day when she'd been there and nodded to them again. They'd been in and out of her shop for weeks now. They were all flirts and most of them needed their heads bashed in. She was sure some woman was going to do it to each of them, too. Stormy left them to their teasing each other and talked to the men at the trucks.

"Mr. Smith said you were to get them all. Told us to tell you if you could see your way to putting a little tent sign on them to say where you got them, he'd be much obliged." She told him she could do that. He handed her some little stand up advertising. "He said he'd do the same for you. And if you'd be so kind as to send your aunts to him whenever you want, he'd like that too. I think he's sort of sweet on them."

Storm looked at her aunts. They were laughing with the Harrison family and having a good time. She never forgot how much they'd given up to take her in, and it occurred to her how old they were beginning to look. Turning back to the man, he explained to her how to take the straps off the tables. She just let him talk. Sometimes it was just easier to let them explain than to tell them she knew how to do things on her own.

There were ten tables of varying ages, as well as fifty chairs. One of the tables, she'd been told, had been broken when it was being loaded, so she was short one. Storm had no idea how she was going to get ten tables in her little shop, much less all the chairs.

"Put the sturdy ones outside." Storm looked at Bri, then back at the front of the shop. "You don't have to serve them, just make it possible for them to have a seat should they want it. And you'll need some pretty planters, too. Nothing says homey better than a pot of flowers. You should also put in window boxes. They'll freshen it up, too."

"I'm not really the making things homey type." Bri laughed and told her she'd help her. When she also mentioned an awning, Storm let her plan. She was as bad as her aunts in making more work for themselves. People could just take the stuff home and eat it as far as she was concerned.

It was a good idea, her Aunt Sally said, and a great way to bring in more business in the warmer months. The flowers could be watered easily enough, and there was plenty of room for two tables with a couple of chairs each. Unloading the trucks, Bri picked out the ones she thought would be the best, and they moved from there.

All the tables fit but one. It ended up going up the stairs to Danny's new place, because she knew for a fact that he didn't have one. The bed that had been dug up for him a couple of days before was taken up as well. Bri sent one of the boys home for two dressers that she had in storage, and Danny was all set. He even told her that he'd keep the plants up when she got them planted for her helping him out.

Ordan ran to the market and picked up some luncheon meats and things to make sandwiches. When he returned twenty minutes later, she had the bread sliced as well as some homemade honey mustard whipped up. Her aunts said that they'd watch the place while she made up a large serving tray of assorted sandwiches. Ordan had even picked up some chips and several different kinds of salads, such as potato and macaroni. Taking eating utensils to the new tables, Bri suggested that the bakery might serve sandwiches, too. Her aunts had been saying the same thing for days now.

"I'll tell you what, you come in and make them for me and I'll have lunch served, too. Aunt Lynn makes the best cucumber salad you've ever eaten, and Aunt Sally can make anything you want with pasta. Her cold mac and cheese salad is out of this world."

"Deal." She had no idea why, but Storm had expected Bri to turn her down. She was happy and a little nervous about having her around so much. What if this thing with Riordan fell apart? Then what? "You'll bake the bread, right? And make this mustard sauce?"

"I can do that. But if you don't mind, we should start out small. That way if it doesn't work out, we won't have a lot of stuff invested in it." Bri laughed. "You have something else in mind?"

"Yes. I think that once word gets around that you're serving lunches like this one, you're going to be too busy to get away even for a day."

Aunt Lynn came to the table and grinned. Storm could only imagine what she was going to say to her.

"Those two guys up there at the counter want to know if they can have a boxed lunch like you're having to go. I told them that it was going to be ten dollars, but they said they'd pay twice that to have a lunch that good looking." Bri just grinned at her. "You think we can do that?"

They ended up selling seventeen sandwiches and taking orders for a dozen more for tomorrow. Bri could not contain her excitement. Storm didn't even tell her that she'd be making her own money at this venture, minus the cost of the bread and bags. Storm just knew that there would be an argument and she was in too good a mood to spoil it with a fight. And it would be, too, with Bri. She had a stiff backbone that she rarely let people see.

# CHAPTER 8

Riordan walked around the living room and wondered why Storm didn't live here. The house was set up, beautifully maintained, and even had a staff on duty at all times. As they made their way to the upper floors, he looked at the portraits hanging from long chains, one right after the other.

"Relatives?"

Stormy nodded but didn't say anything else. The man that was leading them up the long curved staircase reminded him of a butler from a classic movie...starched and stiff, and wearing his uniform like it was part of his body. And he was English, if Riordan's ears had heard correctly. He also thought the man was very nervous about having the lady of the house, as he had called Storm, in residence.

"This is the master suite. As you can see, things have been left alone, my lady, just as you requested." She nodded, and Riordan saw that she was uncomfortable. Whether it was her being referred to by the title "lady" or the house in general, he didn't think she wanted to be there.

*Could you ask him to leave us alone?* Storm looked at him, then at the butler. *Please? I'd like to talk to you and he's not going to like your answer to me, I think.*

"Anderson, can you give us a few minutes please? Let Margaret know that Mr. Harrison and I will be staying for dinner. Thank you." As he left them, Riordan moved toward her and pulled her to his body. "You have something to say to

101

me that's going to piss me off? I'm not in the mood right now."

"You hate this place, don't you?" She didn't say anything but moved away from him and to the window. "Why did you want me to see it if you hate it so much?"

"I didn't. Aunt Sally wanted you to see it. And I don't hate this place, but find it cold and unfriendly. Even when I lived here as a child, I didn't like the way the house seemed to close in on me." She sat on the window seat and looked around the room as she continued. "The only other time I've been in this room was just after my parents died. Anderson brought me in here to ask me what I wanted to keep or toss. I told him what you heard, just to leave it alone until I told him to take care of it. I still don't have a clue what the fuck to do with this shit. My parents lived here for their entire marriage, and I knew less about them than I do your parents in the month I've known them."

"It's only a house." She told him she knew that. "No, I mean it's not a home, it's just a house. My parents' place is a home. There are pieces of all of us all over the place. Pictures and things we made for them as kids. You should see our Christmas tree. It's covered in toys we picked up, things we made for Mom in school, and pictures. Mom takes a picture of us every year, frames it, and puts it on the tree with the date on it."

"The last tree I remember having here was put up by a decorator and taken down by the same crew. I was never allowed to put a single thing on it, and if I tried to sneak something in, Mother would take it off and tell me that it was for the guests that came by and not children." He felt his heart break for her. "They were never cruel to me. I didn't get beaten or sent to my room because of some small infraction. They loved me in a way, I guess, but I was an ornament that was brought out during parties for a few minutes, then sent to the nursery."

"How old were you when they died?" He sat beside her on the bench. He could see a covered pool and a pool house, as well as a large barn that looked freshly painted. The lawns were perfectly ordered, and he'd bet anything that there was a garage somewhere on the property that would have cars, older ones, stashed away in it.

"Eleven, nearly twelve. They were both in the same accident, but they didn't die at the same time. Mother died instantly and my father died a week later. I always thought that he'd been too stubborn to die first and wanted to make sure that he stayed the longest. I have no idea why...like I said, they weren't bad parents, just unemotional. I think that's why I enjoy yours so much." He nodded. Riordan knew that both his parents loved Storm and could not wait for her to stop calling them Mr. and Mrs. "I want to show you my room."

As they moved down the long hallway, he saw more pictures. He wanted to ask her if they were really all related to her when he came upon a picture of a woman and had to stop and stare. Storm moved up beside him and smiled.

"My great-great-great grandmother. She is said to have been a hellion. My aunt used to tell me that she went hunting with her husband one year and bagged the biggest bear. I always thought that I'd have liked her a good deal more than my own mom." Riordan thought that the two of them would have loved each other, and the trouble that they would have gotten into together would have been legendary. "I look like her, don't I?"

"You could be her twin." He noticed the necklace she had on and had to laugh. "Is that a bear's claw she is wearing?"

"It is. I have it in my room. Or I used to. I don't know what's in there any longer." As they started down the hall again, he could tell that she wasn't as sad about the place. Even her walk seemed to be—Riordan stopped walking and watched her walk down the hall in front of him.

"Storm, how do you feel?" He was almost afraid to have her answer him. He was excited yet afraid it was all in his imagination, too. When they'd made love last night, he'd touched her body and had felt the scars and thought they were smaller, but he'd fallen asleep.

"Fine. Why do you ask? You want to fuck me in my old room?" Her giggle had him thinking that a lot of things had changed in the last several days. She was relaxed more, her temper was slower to flare up, and she was smiling more. "What is it, Riordan?"

Instead of answering her, he took her into the first room he found. He knew it was her room as soon as he looked around. It was what he would have expected from the woman in front of him as a child. But right now he wanted to see if he was right.

"Take off your clothes." She grinned at him again, then frowned. "I need to see your body. I know that you hate to look at yourself, but I love the feel of your skin. I know every inch of you. But right now, I need to look at you."

Her pants came off first. Riordan didn't touch her, even though every part of him wanted to tear her clothing off and look at her. But when she pulled her shirt up and over her head and stood in front of him, he knew that he was right. When she turned as he asked her to do, Riordan had to hold onto the bed that he was near.

"You're healing." She turned and looked at him when he spoke. He thought she'd not heard him so he said it again. "The scar on your back is nearly gone. The smaller ones are gone completely. And your legs are stronger, too. I can see the muscle tone is back; your calf is thick with muscles."

"I don't understand."

But he did. And he was pretty sure that's what his dad had been trying to tell him the other day. He'd said that she was working too hard now, that she should take it easy until she was used to her body again. Again. He knew that she was getting her body back. Riordan moved toward her slowly. He was afraid that when he got close enough, he'd see that he'd been wrong. But the scars were fading and her body was stronger.

"When you bite me, you take some of my blood into your body. It's strong. I can heal with just a shift. I think that it's healing you." He touched his fingers to the scar on her back, much like he had the first time he'd touched her. "This one was wider, and as long as my hand. It's not that now. I'd say that it's less than three inches and only about an eighth of an inch wide. The smaller ones are gone, not even pink."

He turned her in his arms so that he was facing her now. She looked afraid, and he didn't blame her. Riordan was slightly afraid himself.

"Am I a tiger then?" He shook his head, and his cat moved along his skin as if to say, hey, but we can fix that. Calming him, because she was so afraid, Riordan begged his cat to let him handle this. "I can feel him. He's right there, isn't he?"

"Yes. He wants you." She turned and looked at him. "I've wanted to let him mark you for days now. He wants to taste you, too."

"You mean...you don't mean he wants to have oral sex with me, do you?" Riordan kissed her shoulder and rocked into her pussy. He wanted to have oral sex with her, too, but one thing at a time. "Will he want to have sex, too?"

"No. Just taste you and then mark you." She leaned back into his chest, and Riordan cupped her breast by lifting her bra out of the way. "If you lay down on the bed, right now, I'll shift and he can have you."

She moved from him. Riordan thought for sure she was going to hit him, but all she did was move to the bed. When she sat down then stood up, he was so disappointed that he nearly sobbed. But all she did was remove her panties and her bra. When she lay back down, he pulled his borrowed tee-shirt over his head and dropped it on the floor.

"I'm going to shift. Will that frighten you?" She only snorted at him. "Yeah, I guess not. Then you have to do me a favor…don't run. If you do then we'll chase you down, and your staff is not going to like that."

"I have one request." He nodded. Right now he'd give her anything. Even have a baby for her. "Will you help me make this place a home? Like your parents'? Can we get married here, have children and raise them as little hellions without maids or nannies?"

"We'll need help with nannies, love. I'm not going to have you exhausted all the time when I want you. And after I change you, if you want, I want to be able to run with you for hours without having to worry about the children."

"I want to be your cat." He nodded and pulled his pants off. He was stiff and hard, his cock so full that he was thinking that one taste of her was going to be all he could do. But he let his cat take him and watched her.

"You're beautiful." His cat moved forward slowly. His big head was bigger than her entire waistline, and he didn't want to hurt her. Her fingers in his fur behind his ears had the big animal purring, and she hugged him to her. "I don't know what to do."

*Lay back and spread your legs.* She did that but didn't move fast enough for his cat. Pressing his large body between her legs, he buried his head over her pussy and inhaled deeply. Riordan could smell how aroused she was, too. And when he licked her, Storm came up off the bed.

"Christ, that was wonderful." Without him telling her, she lay back, this time spreading her legs wide. "Eat me, Riordan. Please, eat me."

~~~

Storm felt his tongue touch her in ways that no one had before. His tongue was rough and long; it was strong, too, and when he curled it around her clit she came, crying out his name. Holding him to her, she rode his tongue as he fucked her with it. His teeth touched her sometimes but never enough to hurt her. When she came again, this time using the pillow on her bed to cover her screams, she felt him lick her thigh and waited for the pain. Instead of pain, however, she felt something akin to a tightening. Looking down at where he had his teeth deep in her thigh, she asked Riordan what was happening.

*My saliva numbs it for you. I've never done this before, but I thought, like you apparently did, that it would hurt.* The big tiger lifted his head and growled at her. Then he was Riordan. *My turn.*

His mouth seemed to be everywhere. His hands and fingers massaged and touched her in places that she was sure no one had touched her before. His mouth ate at her, ate her like she was his feast and he was going to gorge himself on her. When his fingers slid into her, curling around until she felt him touch something wild and dark in her, she screamed again, her body bowing up off the bed until she thought she was going to come apart. When he pulled her off the bed and onto his cock, Storm wrapped herself around him.

"Christ, you taste delicious. I could eat you all day and never get enough." Riordan lifted her up by her ass and lowered her over and over until she thought she was going to die from the pleasure of it. And when he rolled them over and had her on her back, she held onto him like she was going to fly away.

"I want to bite you, too." He nodded and tilted his head for her. She could see his pulse there, pounding hard against his skin. Her mouth watered to sink her teeth into him, but she waited, knowing that it was important to bite when they came. But the thought of the taste of him, the need to taste all of him, had her scraping her teeth over him, and he cried out that he was coming.

Storm bit down and tore his skin as blood, hot and spicy, filled her mouth. Her own climax grabbed her seemingly by the throat, and held her suspended for several seconds until it dropped her over the large cavern. And she didn't land so much as she simply came to rest at the end of the great fall.

Storm woke alone in the bed. Riordan wasn't in the room with her, and his clothing was gone. Getting up, she made her way to the bathroom and knew that he'd made use of it, too. The stall was wet with small droplets of water, and his towel was hanging crookedly over the handle of the shower door. There was a note on the counter, which she picked up to read.

"My dearest darling...too mushy? Yeah, I thought so, too. I'm down in the kitchen. Or the office if you have one here. I'm going to need bread crumbs to find my way around. I love you, Storm. I truly do."

She stared at the last line for several seconds before putting it down and turning on the water. Surely he was just saying that. No one loved her. Laughing, she got under the spray and washed up. It was then that she noticed that her skin felt softer, the muscles more full. She had to lean against the wall to let her breathing get back under control.

*Are you all right?* Storm screamed at the sound of his voice. *I'm sorry, love, but I could feel how upset you were. Do you want me to come up there?*

*No. I'm fine. I just realized what you said is right. I'm healing.* He told her that he was coming up. *No, really, I'm fine. I'm nearly done now. I'll...did you find the office?*

*Yes. And I love it. Did you know that there are books in here older than some I've seen in museums? And this desk...where the hell did you get this thing? It has more drawers in it than all my dressers at my apartment.* She smiled at him as she dried off. *Oh, and Anderson said that there have been inquiries about what you plan to do with this place. What do you want to do with this place? Because if you really want to turn it into a home, I'm all for it. I love this house.*

*The desk, it was a former president's, I think. I don't know which one, but Anderson more than likely knows. And the office was my father's. Though now that I think about it, I don't think he ever used it except when he had company.* She had to laugh. *Riordan, what do you think about going from room to room and tossing what we don't want in order to start over? I don't have any attachment to this stuff except a few pieces.*

*So long as I can keep this desk, I'm okay. And the chair. Oh, and the leather ones by the fireplace in here. Can I keep the conference table, too? And the...maybe you should just come down here and let me show you.* She was nearly down the stairs when he spoke again. *I need you to come to the office, please. I think we might have an issue.*

Hurrying now, she made her way to the back of the house. When she got there, she had to make her way through the staff that was crowding into the room with Riordan. Storm made her way to him as she asked what was going on.

"Lady Browning, we were wondering if you were planning to sell." She looked at the rest of the staff when Anderson spoke. Some she knew, most she didn't. "We've been loyal servants all this time and think we should know as soon as possible if we are to find other employment."

"Do you want to find other employment? And before you answer that, you should know that we're thinking about living here. But there will be changes. I'm not my parents' daughter, and I won't do what they did here." She thought she saw relief on Anderson's face, but it was there and gone so fast that she wasn't sure. He asked her what sort of changes she might want to have. "Well, for one thing, I want to get rid of the furniture in the grand room. It's...well, it's not fun."

"Yes, I can see that." Storm was surprised by his agreement. "I would like to suggest that you redo the kitchen as well. I'm not the cook in there by any means, but it does not flow well if you should entertain. And I'm assuming that you will be entertaining now that you're here?"

"All right. I can do that. But as far as entertaining goes, I don't know about that. We'll have family over, I suppose. And holidays. I don't know much about holidays, but I want my own tree." He nodded, then looked around the room they were in. "This room stays the way that Mr. Harrison wants it. If he wants it gone, then okay, but no moving this room."

"Yes, my lady." Anderson grinned at her as he moved deeper into the room. "We have kept up with you. All of us have. I should like to show you something."

Nodding, she waited while he took a book from the bottom shelf of the bookshelf. It was thick and old looking, but well cared for. Riordan came around the desk to look at it with her when Anderson handed it to her.

"I would go to find newspapers when we heard you were in them." The woman that stepped forward curtsied. "I'm the cook, miss. June Price is my name. I didn't work here when your parents lived here. I should very much like to stay if you mean to keep the house. All of us would. We think of you as our own, you see."

She could see that. The book was filled with clippings from the newspapers. Some of them weren't even in English, but she knew they were about her, including the one where she'd been hurt. It didn't mention her name, but it was there. She looked at Anderson.

"Mr. Blackson kept us updated on your progress. He said that there would be no mention of you for safety reasons, but he did send us reports and the newspapers when he could find them." He nodded to the desk. "He called us just a while ago. Told us that you'd met a man and that you might be moving here. We've been getting ready, I suppose you could say, hoping for a time when you returned home."

"This was never my home." He nodded and told her he knew that. "Mr. Harrison and I might get married, but we do want to make this our home, not a house."

"It's never been a home. But we will gladly help you make it one." She nodded, too, moved by their support to do much more than that. "Now then. We shall have dinner at six. Will there be just the two of you this evening? I'm to understand that you have a rather large family, Mr. Harrison.

If you should like to invite them now, we'd have plenty of time to prepare for their arrival."

"I'll call them now and see if they can come to visit." He looked down at her as Riordan continued talking to Anderson. "I'd like for you to contact Lady Browning's aunts, if you don't mind, and see if they can join us as well."

"Very good, sir. Also, I shall set them up a room or two as well. There is no reason for them to travel back if they should like to stay over." Anderson moved the staff out of the room but paused at the doorway. "If you do not mind me asking, what took you so long, my lady?"

"I don't know, Anderson. I just don't know." He nodded, and she stopped him once more. "Could you do me one more favor please? Call a contractor in the morning and have the entire kitchen updated, as well replacing appliances that need it. And see that your home is renovated too. Does Mrs. Price live here, too? If so, see that she has what she needs as well."

After they were gone, she wrapped her arms around Riordan. He kissed the top of her head and then lifted her chin up so that she could see him. His smile made her think he was enjoying this.

"Not one *fuck* or *shit* the entire time you were talking to them. Could it be that you might be civilized after all?" She told him to fuck off. "Ah, there's my girl. So, we're living here, now?"

"If you're sure you want to." He picked her up and sat with her on his lap at the big desk. "I still want to work. Go to the bakery every day and make things."

"I think you should. And I'll work, too. But not every day. And I would appreciate it if you didn't work every day either. It's obvious that you can afford it." She nodded. "My parents are coming, by the way. As are my brothers. Don't be overwhelmed if my mom tries to help you with the house."

"I won't. I like her and your dad." Storm leaned on his chest as she continued. "I'd like for my aunts to live here, too, if they want. I know that they have a house of their own, but they're not young anymore, and the yard work is a lot for them."

"I was going to suggest it." He held her for a long time, and she felt his breaths rise and fall slowly. "Storm, will you marry me?"

# CHAPTER 9

Tony didn't want to do this today. He had stuff to do, things to be preparing for. But he needed to make them aware of what was going on, as soon as possible. But when he pulled into the big drive, he changed his mind. Today, he discovered, was a day for family. He nearly turned around and drove off, but Mac came out of the house to greet him.

"It's family here now. I can come back tomorrow." Mac put his arm around him and led him to the big front of the house. "Seriously, one more day won't make that much difference."

"Sure it will. You came all the way here to warn them about something...I can see it on your face. And the best time to warn family is when they're all together. Come in and have some dinner. I'm sure there will be plenty, and if not, then you'll have to starve. Because as good as the smell is coming from that kitchen, I'm not going to give you any portion of what's mine." Tony nodded, knowing that he'd just blow off dinner with them and get this over with quickly. "Tony, are they in trouble?"

"She is. And I would think your brother is, simply because he'll not leave her to do this on her own." Mac nodded this time as they made their way to the big dining room. The table was being set, dishes were being argued over, and he had to smile. "She'll get her way...Mrs. Harrison. She always does."

113

"I'm letting her win this time because she had a good point. Hello, Tony. You'll join us, yes?" He didn't answer but did ask about the argument. "She thinks that these dishes are ugly, but I do not. But when she explained to me their origin, I have to agree now. I'm going to use them at the bakery for my luncheons. That way, if they are broken, no one cares."

He thought them ugly, too, but said nothing about them. He'd been eating meals from a tray for so long that he wasn't sure that he'd know what to do with a set of dishes. And a coffee cup that didn't have as many chips as it did stains. When Storm came back in the room, he asked to speak to her and Riordan for a moment. She took him to an office that was bigger than his entire apartment.

"My father's, but Riordan is going to make it his own. And the house, too. Thank you for seeing to it while I tried to…whatever it was I was doing." Tony told her it was his pleasure. "I'd forgotten how big this place is, and how cold."

"I had no idea you came from this much. You never said. The first time I came here, I thought for sure I had the wrong address." Riordan said nothing, but Tony could tell that while the place was bigger than the one that his family had, he saw it as nothing more than a place to rest his hat. Even by military standards, this place was huge and had a wealth that he'd bet went back for several generations. "I have to talk to you about some things. You might want to brief Riordan's family later, but for now, I'm going to tell you what we know."

He laid five pictures in front of them when they sat at the long oak table. It was polished to a high sheen, and the grain in the wood was beautiful. Tony sat down in the chair across from them and asked Storm if she knew any of the men in the photos. This wasn't what he wanted to be doing, but he'd been sent by someone higher on the food chain than him.

"Yes. All of them. They were the last thing we were assigned before the accident. I never got to…it wasn't anything I was involved in before that, and after…well, I never went back." He nodded. "They're coming for me, aren't they?"

"Yes. Well, some of them are. They don't know who you are as yet, but I have a feeling that that won't be long in coming. This one is calling himself the Viper." He pointed to the middle picture. "The others have similar names. These two are Bear and Demon, for whatever reason. And these two on the end are Massacre and Destruction. These latter two are dead. Killed five days ago at an airport here in the States. We are looking to see how they got in and where they were headed, but a woman at the airport recognized their faces and made a call to my office. I had nine men, all out going, there at the same place, and they took them out."

"Out going?" Tony had forgotten that Riordan wouldn't be up on their language and explained. "So you had men there that just happened to be going back overseas, and they just happened to be armed to do this."

"Yes." He waited for the man to ask more. He was smart and he'd know things that wouldn't come to most civilians. When Riordan looked at Storm, she smiled at him.

"Like police, Special Forces are on duty at all times. And I would imagine that these men weren't really going out, but just making it appear that way. In most all larger airports there are people like this patrolling all the time. It's what keeps you safe." Tony neither agreed nor disagreed with what Storm just said, but Riordan nodded as if he understood the reason for it all.

"So what makes you think that they're after Storm? Maybe there is someone else that they were targeting." Tony lay the final picture on the table. It was blood stained, having been taken from one of the deceased. It was an old, somewhat blurry picture of Storm when she was in country. She was standing next to two of her men, and her face was bright with laughter. "Who took this?"

"That's what we need to find out." Storm picked the picture up. "I'm here to ask you if you are sure all of your men were killed that day."

She didn't even flinch from the question, and he knew that she'd been thinking the same thing. But the longer she stared at the photo, the more nervous he became. Riordan got up and went to the door, and in a few minutes someone brought in a tray of drinks, as well as a platter of cheese and crackers. He took the drink but declined the food. When she laid the picture down, he could see she was upset.

"We were leaving for the last ride. I had just told a joke about…well, it's not a very nice joke, and there are times when I can't believe I said some of those things. But we were stressed and it helped to calm us. But one of them pulled out a cell and snapped us. I was stunned at first when he stood there with the phone, and when I took it from him, he didn't fight me when I put a round in it." Riordan asked her why she'd done that. "We weren't allowed to have them. Not at all. Not just because we couldn't be talking on it when we should be working, but for the exact reason that he used it for. We were elite and our faces were never known. He sent it to someone, didn't he?"

"We think so. It took us a while to figure it out. Since you destroyed the phone, it will be harder to figure out who received the picture. Then someone in the office got the bright idea to try and narrow down where it was taken. After that, it was a piece of cake to see what phones in that area sent something out. It's not the only one that he took and sent out. There were pictures of all of you. But mostly you." Storm got up to pace, and Tony continued. "Ten days ago, this surfaced on the Internet. I wasn't made aware of it until five days ago, after the shooting at the airport. Since then, I've had a team looking into seeing if there were more of them. There are four that we've found of you. Ten more of the team. And two of the day that you were bombed."

"Have you found him yet?" He told her he had not. "Then you're sure that it's Malcom Brewer? I mean, no doubt at all."

"Not until this very moment, no, I wasn't sure. Why do you think it's him? Besides the phone, I mean?" He wanted to know her reasoning. A phone was nothing. Any one of them could have taken this picture and the others, and it had little to do with Brewer. But she'd worked with him and the others for years; she'd know him better than anyone.

"He had money." He nodded. Tony knew that as well. His accounts had had a huge flux of money going in and out prior to the bombing, and now they were empty, closed out three days after they had picked up Storm. "I think I had a feeling then, and I was going to say something to someone, but we were going out again and I'd…I guess I just didn't want to believe it. Have you contacted his wife?"

"Dead." She nodded as if she might have known that. "His house has been sold, as have the cars he had here as well. Cash, so there was no tracking the money. Nothing is paid off in the form of his loans, credit cards, or nothing."

"Why would he if you thought he was dead?" Tony looked at Riordan when he spoke. "I'd look offshore if you haven't already. He'd have to have somewhere to stash the money. And in my experience in dealing with people who are cheats, once a liar always one. And the people he was working for more than likely know that as well."

"So you think that whoever he sent the picture to is more than likely thinking that he'll go against them as well?" It had been considered around the team, then dismissed when he pointed out a few things to them. Most of it was speculation, and others…well, they dismissed it, and he was glad for it. "What else could he give them after the pictures? That's what has us stumped."

Instead of answering his question, Riordan pointed to the pictures of the men. "These men, they're not American. Won't blend in. They more than likely have attitudes that will make them stand out. I've worked with some other foreign

117

companies that continued to fail no matter how many times we tried to help them because of their morals and ways they did things, such as the way they treated women in their business. These men would have much of the same ground into their heads." Tony nodded. "This Brewer person, I'm assuming he's the boy next door type. Blond, blue eyed or something like that. Probably has an accent."

Storm laughed. "Yeah. Texas. And he had green eyes with the reddest hair you've ever seen. Called him Red for the first year, but we finally had to stop when we got a guy on the team that was actually called Red. So you think he's just like one of the guys, could be here already, telling them all about me."

Tony watched Riordan. He was a great deal like Storm in that he didn't think aloud but thought things through. He watched his face for any kind of tell, but there wasn't any. And just like Stormy, Tony would never play poker with this man. He wanted answers, damn it.

"He's more than likely living and working right in this town. And reporting back to whoever it is that is looking for you right now." Tony had thought so, too. "Now that we know this, we can fight back. Get his scent. Make sure the family and anyone else around us that can help track his whereabouts sees his picture. We sniff him out, quite literally."

"I have a team coming here." Storm was shaking her head while Riordan was nodding. "They're part of the team that you've worked with before. You'd be in charge of them."

"I'm not ready to be in charge yet." He thought she'd been ready the day she was released from the hospital, but thought that saying that now would piss her off more. "Fuck, Tony, I'm just getting my life back in shape. Why do I want with a bunch of pussies working under me?"

"Yeah, Burkhardt said the same about you." It was a long shot and one that could get the man killed, and Burkhart no more wanted to work with Storm than she did him. But they were perfectly matched when it came to working. And Tony needed to have Burkhardt watching over Storm for him. "He said he'd rather the shooter came to him about getting you dead. Not his exact words, but close enough."

"Yeah?" He nodded. "You're so full of shit. Did you really think you could play me like that? Come on, I'm not that stupid. He may not like me, but he'd never tell you to let me be dead. No more than I would him. I might want to pull the trigger, but never would I let him die. Where is he now? On the property, I'm betting."

Tony laughed. Of course she'd know it. "He is. As are most of his team. They took a hit last week and three are out. Not as badly as yours, but bad."

"Have them investigated, too." He nodded, thinking that she'd be right to want that after this, but he'd already had them looked over. It had been done quietly and privately. "And I've been thinking about something else, too. Danny. I want you to see into his background. It's just too pat that he'd come work for me just as this shit is going down." Tony was surprised by that but said nothing.

"I had him looked into when I found out that he was working for you." She told him to look harder. Making a note to do so, he watched her pace again. "No one but a few know that you're involved with the Harrisons. And I'd bring your aunts here, too. No point in letting them be used against you. As well as I've put some people on the Harrison home as well."

"I'll take care of them. Call them off. I have someone that owes me, and I'll talk to him. Also, I'd like for you to not come back here. Not that I don't trust you, but you could be hurt in this." He nodded. Tony had already thought of that as well. He wanted no one to get hurt in this unless it was by his order. And he wasn't ready to order that just yet. He was doing this by the books, his books.

As she continued, he made notes. Riordan was making them as well, and when he got up and left them, Storm sat down. She was going to tell him something that he was pretty sure he didn't want to know.

"I have two friends that I'm going to bring in to work with Burkhart. When they get here, he's going to pitch a fit. But I need to be sure about several things, and these guys can do it." He asked her if he knew them. "I don't think so. Both are vamps that I've worked with before. They're not nice, rarely have anything nice to say, and are fucking bastards when they don't get their way."

"All right." He stood up. "I'm going to leave you my drop phone number. I know you know the drill, but don't use it more than once, and when you do, I'll send you the new number."

"I won't call you. I'll send someone." He nodded, almost afraid to ask her who it would be, but didn't get the chance when someone was suddenly in the room. "This is Mason. Don't fuck with him and he won't fuck with you."

After shaking hands with the man, he knew why he wasn't to fuck with him. He was an old and very powerful vampire, despite looking like he was only about twenty, if that. When the man demanded a taste, Tony wasn't sure he wanted to give it to him, but Storm told him that was the only way she would work with him.

The small bite wasn't painful, but Tony knew that forever this man would be right there with him. Maybe not physically, but he'd know his every mood, his every thought, and where he was at all times. That could either be good or deadly. Tony wasn't looking forward to finding out. A short time later, they were all sitting down to dinner together, and that was when Burkhardt showed up.

~~~

Viper moved along the woods. He had been here several times in the last few days, and not once had he seen the woman or the man that was supposed to be this great love of hers. And he could no longer rely on his inside man to help him. The man had served his purpose, and now he was as good dead, which, to Viper's way of thinking, should have happened months ago.

"She's not here." No kidding, he wanted to tell the man on the phone connection in his ear. "I don't think she's coming in while I'm around the building. I'm thinking that she's got this guy to fuck now, and the business ain't appealing as it was before. He's got himself some big bucks."

Viper didn't tell him that Browning could have bought and sold Harrison several times over, but then he was never one to tell all that he knew. Instead, he watched the building for the old women. Why they weren't under some male's control was beyond him. Women were not to be left on their own. It was high time that Browning knew that as well. And he was going to take them today or know the reason why.

When the large vehicle pulled up in front of the building, Viper watched the men get out.

Military. He'd know that even if he didn't see the guns they carried and the way they were dressed. They had a way about them that told him that they'd been trained and trained well. And they would never balk at killing someone if they needed to. Dead was better than living and wounded.

It was then that he saw her. The picture that he'd been given all those months ago had done little to tell him that she was beyond beautiful. He already knew that she was smart and cunning. Viper had made it his business to know all there was to know about the woman. What he knew about her, however, was very little compared to what he knew was yet to be found. The man that thought he was directing this take down of the woman had no idea what kind of plans Viper had for her. Nor did he think she'd be answering any of his questions.

Like, where did she learn to fight like a man? Someone had done her a great disservice to train her like one of them. And he was going to find that person as soon as she was his. He didn't want to have her as a wife. Now that he could see her it was tempting, but she was not his type. He liked his woman more subservient and mindful of their place. Viper knew that no matter how many times he beat her, Browning would forever be the wrong kind of woman for him.

And where had her information come from that led to the bombing of his home? There was no way that she'd figured this out on her own. Women did not have the intelligence to do something like that. He'd been told that she'd been the one to order the airstrike, as well as the elimination of the men that had not been killed by the blasts. They had been lined up and murdered like they were nothing more than dogs that ran the streets.

She was slightly smarter than most women he knew, but she would not have been able to figure out where to bomb them. And she'd known that he was living there, that he'd been on the compound when it had happened. Someone was helping her.

"The aunts are leaving the building. I think they're onto us." Viper wanted to go to the man's hiding place—which was in plain sight as far as he was concerned, and he should have been found out weeks ago—and kill the man. He was giving him updates on things that he could see as plainly as he could see his own battered and burned hand.

The two older women came out of the building, and even if he had wanted to make them dead for even being related to Browning, there was no chance of it happening. They were well surrounded, in addition to the fact that they did not move as one unit as he'd seen done in this country. They moved as if they wished to be a moving target, one that would be difficult to catch. When the Browning woman paused before getting into the vehicle, he stilled.

She was looking right at him, or at the very least in his direction. As she stood there watching, he tried his best not to move back deeper into the shadows, not to breathe too loudly, even though there were ten yards or more between them. When she took a step in his direction, then another and another, he slowly moved his hand down to his weapon and put his hand over the butt of it. When she stopped, so did he.

There were less than five yards between them now. A mere fifteen feet separated him from his prey. The woman that had nearly brought his entire army to ruin, the bitch that did not die when she should have, was close enough to him that he could see the color of her eyes. When she started forward again, he pulled his weapon free of the holster at his side and held it down. This time when she stopped, he could see the smirk on her face and hated her all the more for it and her arrogance.

"I have your scent now, Viper." The skin on the back of his neck danced. His heart began to pound all the harder for the quiet deadliness of her words. "I'm coming for you, fuck wad. And when I find you—and there is no doubt that I will—you are going to suffer terribly at the hands of a woman. How does that make you feel?"

Viper wanted to shoot her then. Fire upon her body until she was nothing more than a mass of blood on the ground. But men came to stand beside her, too many for him to kill and get away. And Viper would get away. Going back to his father to tell him what he'd done was all he lived for.

She stood there for several more minutes. He knew that should anyone take two more steps toward him, just small ones at that, he'd be found. Viper was sure of nothing else except that he did not want to be caught on American soil after what he had done to so many.

Her laughter accompanied her as she backed away. The men went with her, their guns at their shoulders, their aim on his location even though he was fairly sure that none of them could see him. But at her command, he also knew that they'd fire until they hit him, and then it would be over. Viper marveled at her smooth steps back, her innate ability to see where she stepped without looking, and the way that she was as confident as if she were positive that he was right where she was looking.

Viper knew then that he was going to enjoy killing her more than he'd ever thought possible. And when he did, he was going to make sure the world knew that he'd done it. He would be the most wanted man in the world when he was finished with the bitch Browning.

Moving back into the building that he'd been using for weeks now after they left, he knew that there would be no way he could return here. Looking around, he didn't see anything that would indicate that he'd been here, or anyone for that matter, but he knew that taking care of the man who worked for him and his cause, as well as her lover, was going to have to be taken care of soon. Since he knew that access to the old women would be nil now, he had to work another angle. And that would mean the men in her life.

# CHAPTER 10

Burkhardt was pissed. Riordan could see that, but he was pissing him off as well. When she answered his question a dozen times, even he knew that she'd been bluffing when she'd told Viper she could smell him.

"I don't understand why you didn't just open fire." Good question the first four times he'd asked her, but she had already told him why. But when she stood up, he could see that this time was going to be an entirely different answer.

"And when we went in there and it was a bunch of kids fucking around in the building, getting high, having sex, what then? I shoot the shit out of them, or you did, and then what the fuck do you think would have happened then? Huh? Would you be there with me when we had to explain to not only the police and the Feds what I did, but to the families, too? Oh sure, little Pavlov had his pants down around his ankles and his dick in Porsche's ass when they died, because we didn't take the time to fucking check the area properly before we opened fire on a bunch of kids. Guess it sucks to be you. But hey, Burkhardt is fine with that because he's a shit head and doesn't care so long as I tried to kill the bad guy." Burkhardt glared at him when he laughed, but Storm wasn't finished with him as yet. "You are a fucking bastard. Has anyone pointed that out to you?"

"Yes, my wife." If asked, Riordan would have thought a woman would have killed him long ago rather than be married to him, but he did sit down. "Okay, you have a point. But I still want to know why you thought he was there. There had to be something that made you look in that particular place."

"I don't know. I...you know that when Riordan and his brother Aedan went there, they could smell him. And lucky for us the bastard left behind a water bottle that he might have drank out of. We know that the scent on the bottle matches the one where I thought he was. That's more than we had before." Storm got up and went to the makeshift information wall that they'd put up. She didn't turn around as she continued. "We also think that Brewer is in on this somehow. Tony flagged two accounts that he thinks are his. And we have someone watching the bakery."

"Yeah, but we know less than we should going into this thing. For all we know he could be one of your brothers-in-law."

Riordan was out of his seat in seconds, but he should have just stayed where he was. His father had moved, too, and had shifted at the same time. He had Burkhardt down on the floor with his mouth wrapped around his throat, his huge cat pinning him down with his claws in his chest. Storm moved to kneel down next to them.

"I might have forgotten to tell you that my family are tigers. I should have, but then I thought, he'll not say something so stupid that it will get him killed. Or perhaps make him piss his pants when they try to kill him." Storm looked at Riordan, and he went to her. "Riordan, perhaps you can translate what your dad is saying to this fool. And while you're at it, could you also explain to him that I trust my brothers more than I do him right now?"

Riordan sat in the chair and tried not to laugh. His dad was mad, but he was beginning to see the humor in it as well. Storm was something else. She went back to the board as if having a tiger trying to rip the throat out of one of her men was something that happened all the time. He looked at his dad when he said his name.

126

*You should really change her.* He told him he was working on that. *I'm sort of glad today that you hadn't. I'm sure that her temper, and a fine one she has, would have had this man dead and not just...he's trying to speak to you, I think.*

Riordan leaned forward in his chair and looked into the fear-stricken eyes of the lieutenant. He had to look away twice because the man really was terrified, and Riordan was trying his best not to laugh at him.

"You do know that you should have a better care with your comments in this house. I mean, you know that now, right? Blink twice if you do." His eyes blinked twice in such an exaggerated way that he laughed. "And now that you've been introduced to what we are, I'm thinking that you'll take my word for it when I tell you we can protect our own, and that you're only here because Tony wants it that way. By the way, he's a wolf, if you didn't know already."

The eyes blinked one time, and he stared at him with more fear than before. Riordan put his hand on his father's head and rubbed his fingers through the fur. His dad laughed, but Burkhardt whimpered.

"I'm going to have my dad get up and shift back. He'll have to do that in the other room because of your stupidity. He didn't have time to take off his clothing, and they're ripped to shreds. You should have a look at them when he lets you go. That could very well have been you." When his dad told him to behave, Riordan told him he was having fun and that the man needed to learn his place. "And when he comes back in here, you'll apologize to my entire family, and especially him. Do you understand me?"

Burkhardt blinked twice again. That was when Riordan saw the gun at his side. He could have easily used it on his father, and might have even hurt him. But he hadn't, and Riordan had a moment to wonder why until his father lifted his body off the man. His dad's other paw had dug deeply into his arm, and he hadn't been able to move it.

As his dad left the room, Burkhardt sat up. "I'm not usually one that says they were wrong, but I'm terribly sorry for this." Riordan nodded but said nothing. "I don't want to be here. I mean, I want to help, but my wife is ill with our second child, and I'm stressed about leaving her alone again."

"We can have her brought here." He said that she wasn't to travel and it was hard on them right at the moment. "You call her and have her get ready. We'll send someone to get her and to help with the arrangements. If you'll back off a little, maybe we can get this thing finished rather than having to bury you in the back yard. And I will if you say something like that again."

"I understand."

He told him he'd call his wife now and left the room. Riordan watched Darcy and Storm look over the board. He was her fresh eyes, as Aedan had been this morning. When Darcy stood up and took one of the many pictures off the wall and handed it to her, Riordan went to see what he'd found.

"Look at this." Storm took the photo and studied it. "Not the man, Viper, but the entire picture. What do you see?"

When she put the picture on the desk, he looked as well. All he could focus on was the man in the picture and what he was doing. The rest of it was blurred out by the violence of the situation.

Viper was holding a man's head in his hands. It wasn't attached to the body, so other than the dark stain of blood that was dripping from it there was nothing else that he could see. But apparently Storm did, and she looked at Aedan.

"See if you can figure out where this was taken. There are two landmarks here that may help. And I don't want you to share this with anyone." Aedan winked at her and walked away, taking the picture with him. Storm looked at him. "We're in deeper shit than I could have first thought. I need to talk to you later when we're alone, and not before, okay?"

Nodding, he asked her what she'd seen in the photo that no one else had. She only shook her head, and he held her when she wrapped her arms around him. Riordan knew that she was afraid now, but she was also determined. And when his dad came back in the room with the rest of his family, Aedan included, no one mentioned the picture.

"Mom has some stuff she wants us to try. She and that cook of yours, June, have been playing with different kinds of sandwiches all day." Liam set down the tray and picked up one of the several dozen sandwiches. "I'm really liking the beef one, but the ham is really good, too."

Mom came in, too, and had a notepad with a pen. He was glad she was having so much fun at this. But it sucked, too, that she couldn't go back to the bakery until they figured this out. She understood it, but she didn't like it. Neither did Storm or her aunts. They were fretting that they'd need to get something else to help with their income. Riordan had no idea that they had nothing but their pension to get by on every month until this morning, and he felt badly for them.

~~~

Storm was trying her best to listen to the woman who was telling her just what she needed to do with the kitchen. Like she gave a shit. If the refrigerator worked in her old place, that was all she really cared about. But apparently she was missing out on a lot of rebates by not turning in her old things and getting new. When Bri cleared her throat, the design coordinator shut up.

"Maybe if you were to have this conversation with Mrs. Price, as Stormy has suggested several times now." The woman said something about involving her home owners in the selection of the household items. "I'm sure that works well for people who are going to actually use the appliances, but I don't think that Stormy ever will."

"Then she's the one that will be missing out. I don't think I can work under this kind of pressure. All my clients like when I take them step by step through what I'm doing. It saves me time in the long run." For the life of her, Storm had no idea what the woman's name was, but she looked right at her. "Perhaps if you were to get rid of everyone but you and me, we could work this through better."

Storm had had enough. This was the second time that this woman had suggested that she work with her alone, and Storm had things to do. Pulling out her gun from the holster at the back of her pants, she checked to make sure that the clip was full and that there was one in the chamber. Catching the shell as it ejected from the gun, she slipped it in her pocket but held onto the gun.

"Okay, this is what you're going to do, or I'll find someone that will. Talk to June. And if she has some questions, which I highly doubt since she knows her job, then she can come and find me. She won't go on about how the pantry is as old as the house and that the dishwasher is out of date. I know that. It's why I'm having it updated." Storm glanced at Bri and could see that she wasn't upset with the turn of events, but having a hard time not laughing, so Storm continued. "The refrigerator is a relic…yeah, I get that, too. Again, that's why we called someone. You work with her or not at all."

"I cannot work this way." Storm nodded and moved to the kitchen door to open it for her. "You will regret not having Cynthia do your remodeling. I do the homes for all the wealthy. My name means something."

"Not to me." Storm pointed to the door with her gun. "This way, if you please. I've got a shit load of work to do, and you've already eaten up about three hours that I can't get back."

As soon as she was out the door, she seemed to have second thoughts about what she'd just done. "Perhaps we can—"

Storm slammed the door closed in her face. "Who is Cynthia? And why the hell didn't we call her in the first place?"

June patted her on the shoulder as she moved by her. "My lady, that was Cynthia. I've never known anyone to refer to themselves in the first person before. Kind of annoying if you ask me. But now I guess we have to wait on someone else to come out and see what we need to do."

"What is it you were planning to do, June? I mean, were you wanting to enlarge the pantry? Or even to put in a wider refrigerator? I know who can do that for you. If it's simple stuff like that." June handed her a list, and Storm looked it over. "Okay, this is easy. This I can handle."

Picking up the phone, she called the local veterans' office. When she hung up, she had the work covered. As she was making the second call, her aunts came into the room. Bri set about making them a cup of tea each as she told them what was going on. When she hung up, Storm looked at June.

"Nine vets will be here this afternoon to figure out what needs to be done and what stuff will have to be replaced. I want you to send two to your house if you don't mind, and two over to the butler's cottage." June told her that she could do that. "And I've set up an account at the hardware store. You have the final say on anything over five hundred dollars. I really don't want to have to mess with this."

"Very good." June smiled at her. "That's a wonderful idea to get the veterans to work for you. I think they will enjoy this more than what they've been doing at the shelter. Some of them have said they are more suited to hanging wash than to cooking in the kitchen."

Storm moved to the living room with her aunts and Bri and sat on the long couch nearest the fireplace. This room, like their bedroom, was taking on a new look. Most of the furniture in this room had already been replaced with the things from Riordan's apartment, and one of the rooms upstairs now held his bedroom set. For now they were using her room, but a new bed and furniture for the master suite had been ordered and were due to arrive in two days.

"I'd like to talk to you, Storm. We would like to talk to you." Storm told her Aunt Sally she'd wanted to talk to her, too. "The house in town, our house…well, it's in need of some things, too. A new roof. The bedroom where I've been sleeping has more pans on the floor than in our kitchen."

"And the bathroom needs a new commode. The plumber said that he couldn't work on it unless we replaced it with a newer model. He said that kind we have in there is from the twenties and no longer is up to code." Aunt Lynn smiled at her as she continued. "He should have seen the one in the basement. It's the kind that has the pull cord on it, and the tank is attached to the wall."

Bri laughed. "When we had the bathrooms remodeled some years ago, the man told us several times that we should see if the museum would take them from us. I thought that they were doing some remodeling of their own. But he assured me that our things were old enough to be on display. He was quite disturbed that we'd not done anything about it before now."

"I was going to wait on Riordan to be here when I talked to you about this, but he was called away for something and had to go into town for his company. We've talked it over and we want you to come and live here. You should have been staying here while I was gone." Aunt Lynn was shaking her head, and Aunt Sally nodded vigorously. "The house in town will be yours. We'll take care of the plumbing things and give the old girl a once over. You can rent it out after that, or sell it. It would be completely up to you. I've also talked to my bank, and you each now have an account, as well as enough money to take care of anything you need."

"Oh no, love, we can't do that. Your parents left that for you." Aunt Lynn looked at Sally and huffed. "You cannot think to sponge off her. We've gotten by this long without doing so, and we will not do it now that she's home with us."

"That house is costing us more than it's worth and you know it. Why, just last winter, we paid more in monthly heat bills than we did for our house insurance. And you know as well as I do that we had to sit around with blankets piled up to our collective bosom to keep from becoming frozen corpses.

I'd very much like to stay with my grandniece for the rest of my days, rather than to have her come to that monstrosity and find us dead and gone because the tub fell on one of us."

"You can and you will. Had you not taken me in when you did, I would have been put into the system. And I think you'll both agree that I wasn't really a model child." Aunt Sally laughed. Storm did, too. "I was lucky you didn't have me put in a home the day I moved in with you. And now that I'm back, as you have put it, I'm going to take care of you. If you'll let me."

Aunt Lynn leaned back on the couch. "It would be nice to be close to you. But we can't just live here for nothing. We can work, you know. We might be old, but we're far from dead." Aunt Sally told her to speak for herself. "We can put in a garden and do that. You know we need to keep these old bodies moving. The doctor told us that just last month."

Storm looked over at Bri. She was watching her aunts like they were a tennis match. Back and forth her head went. It was funny to see someone else bemused by the two of them. Storm had been living with them forever, it seemed sometimes, but she loved to watch them work through something.

"How long have you been staying with them?" Storm told her since she'd been eleven. "They love you very much. And I'm sure that they'll be moving in."

"Me too. And while they try and see things my way, I have to tell you something, too. I know that we're not really related as yet, but Riordan says that me calling you Mrs. H is driving you insane. I'm sorry about that." Bri laughed. "I'd like to call you Bri if you don't mind. And maybe…well, if you want to think about it some, I understand, but I'd like to someday call you 'Mom.'"

Bri put down her cup and saucer. Storm watched her and wondered if she should have waited for Riordan. But when Bri hugged her to her body, Storm did something she'd not done for years—she hugged her back.

"I'd very much be honored if you would call me Mom. I don't think I've been more touched by something…." She pulled back and looked at her. "You won't mind then? I mean, I know you had a mom and that she passed and all, but she was still your mom."

"'Mom' didn't any more suit her than calling you Mother would. She was Mother, the person that gave birth to me, raised me as required by law, and pretty much stayed as distant from me as one would a skunk." Bri wiped at a tear as Storm continued. "I'm not a girly girl. I don't do shopping unless it's under threat of death, and I hate with all that I am doing the country club thing. I don't play tennis, don't shoot game, unless I need to. And for the love of all that is holy, never ask me to put on a party or tea. You'll be sadly disappointed. However, if you want to learn to shoot a gun, take down an attacker, or to learn how to curse, I'm so there for you."

"I think we can work around that. And speaking of shopping, I received our invitation to the banquet at the White House. It only says that we're invited, but it doesn't say what we're going to." Storm told her that it was a formal thing and that there would be a dinner and some dancing. "That's not what I was asking and you well know it. What is going on that you are avoiding telling me about?"

"It's sort of a—"

Her cell phone vibrated in her pocket, and she excused herself. One look at Bri made Storm think that she'd only dodged the bullet, but the gun was still loaded. Saying her name in the phone, Storm wondered if she could get out of this dinner thing altogether, and knew that it was going to be impossible now.

"What if I told you that I've found something for you that you're going to love me for?" Storm tried to think beyond the feeling that had just hit her. Christ, she was already in love with Riordan. "Baby? Are you there?"

"Yes. I'm here. I was…what did you find?" He laughed and asked her what she was going to give him for the information. "This is not funny. I'm here with your mom and my aunts. There are contractors coming by today to tear up the kitchen at June's say so. We're going to have a mutiny on our hands when my aunts find out how large of a checking account we've set up for them. And you're at work letting me deal with all this alone."

His laughter again warmed her in ways that nothing else had. "I've found some accounts, and Darcy said to tell you that he's found an IP address coming from somewhere close. He's having some trouble pinpointing it. He wants to talk to you about it."

"How much is in the accounts?" Storm had a pretty good idea. Something had been said to her several days ago in passing that had stuck with her. It was why she'd had Darcy helping her with some computer stuff. Not that she couldn't do it herself, but she wanted him to help.

"Fifty-four million, seven hundred and twenty-three thousand, nine hundred and twenty-one dollars and some change." Just what she thought there would be. Almost to the dollar. "There's more too. I think I found the phone records you asked me to find for you. You're not going to believe who they belong to."

"Danny Gunning is one of them, and I'm betting I know who the other one is as well." He told her she was right. And she pretty much knew who had bought them, too.

# CHAPTER 11

Storm moved into the room as silently as a mouse. She knew that Riordan was just outside if she needed him, but for now, she had this. As she moved deeper into the room where she was going to have a seat, she thought about how much fun they'd had today in the living room. Mrs. H...Mom was going to be a big hit when they were able to get the bakery up and going again.

Dressed from head to toe in black and armed with more than she had been in several months, Storm looked around on the desk but didn't hold out much hope of finding anything out where she could see it. Running her hands under the top drawer revealed nothing there either, but she knew that somewhere in this room was a computer that wasn't on the desk. Something that no one was supposed to know about. It took her almost ten minutes, but she finally found it and spoke quietly in the mike at her mouth.

"Got it." The man at the other end laughed at her, and she had to smile. Darcy was having entirely too much fun at this, but she was glad that he knew how. "I have the drive. Tell me when you're ready for me to put the program in for you."

"Is the computer on?" She told him it wasn't. "Then you'll have to start it with the drive in it. That way you don't have to do much more than click a few buttons. Provided that he has no password on it."

As she waited for it to boot up, she looked around the room again from her position on the floor. The computer had been in a false bottom of the bookshelf. Clever if she hadn't herself told him that was where she'd found one stashed once. Darcy said her name.

"You should know that once this is up and running, someone is going to have to man this all the time. While I'm loving helping out, I can't miss that much work. I'm pretty sure that Aedan will murder me." She asked him why. "Because since you and Riordan are a couple, he's not been to work that much and the two of us are doing a lot more. And we have two meetings, two very important meetings tomorrow, and I'm not sure that Riordan is going to leave you for that long."

"I'll make sure that he's there. I need to go into town anyway. I had no idea there was so much involved in upgrading a kitchen. I think that rebuilding the entire fucking house would have been less hassle." The computer made a small sound and she told him what the screen said.

"Okay, hang on a second. I'm checking to see what I can find." The computer was being cloned. The program that Darcy had put on the thumb drive that she was currently trying to load onto the computer would make it so they could see everything that the owner did. And get into his files at the same time. "Um, Stormy, I don't think you're going to need proof to see if he's involved. It's all right here. I'm looking at orders, correspondence between him and some man by the name of Pilchard, and a few between him and a man calling himself Viper. What do you want me to do?"

"Save it. And what you can't figure out, I'll take care of when I get there." He told her he would. "Leave the clone on this. If this doesn't work out tonight, I'll have to keep up on him."

"I have his schedule, too. I'm downloading it as we speak. Christ, there are pictures on here, too. Better ones than you have at the house." She'd already figured out that there might be. As she did a few adjustments on the computer herself, Darcy asked her what she was doing. "You do know if he checks his history, he'll be able to see what you're doing."

"He'll know because I want him to know." She also sent an email to the president. "And if you tell anyone what I'm doing now, I will hunt you down and torture you."

His laughter made her smile. Then she heard from Riordan. *A car is pulling up the drive. Limo with flags. That our boy?*

*Yes. Hide but don't go far.* He told her that he wasn't going anywhere. *And when this is done, and I mean tonight, I want to find a nice quiet place for you to change me. I've had enough of this shit of not being able to talk to all of you. I could have done this without a single noise.*

*I'd love that, but you'll be down for a few days.* He laughed then. *But knowing you, you'll just sit up when I've changed you and demand that I fuck you right now. You'll never do things like I expect, will you?*

*No. What fun will there be in that?* She heard the front door open just as she was putting the computer back, pulled out the thumb drive, and then went to the door. She was going to see if he was alone, and if not, she'd leave the same way she'd come in.

He was alone, and she moved out of the office door into the hall where he was standing. When he turned and saw her, she could see that he was not just surprised to see her, but he was afraid, too. Crossing her arms over her chest, she made sure that he could see that she was armed as well.

"Storm. I suppose that breaking and entering is something that you're used to doing. But it's frowned upon when you do it to your friends." She asked him if they were friends. "Of course we are. You know that."

"Do I? Because the last time I thought of a friend, I never thought of him selling me out. And you did, didn't you, Tony? For fifty-five million...not very much when you think of all the lives that you've fucked up, and the amount of time that was invested in my getting better. But back to the money that you received to give Viper all the information that you could. I remembered that you told me once that there was this island that you were thinking of buying when you retired, and it was just under that dollar amount." He hung up his coat, and she watched to make sure that he wasn't arming himself, too. "Put your hands where I can see them and I won't kill you right now."

"What is it you think you've found? So what, there's an island that is for sale and I mentioned it to you in passing. That means nothing and you know it. You'll have to do better than that, Storm, if you think to bring me down." She saw his wolf move along his skin and was glad that she'd taken the time to find out about silver and what it did to his kind. "I've been really careful. No one, not even the president, knows anything. You don't either. Unless you've caught the rest of my men, and I know for a fact that you haven't."

"The mike is still on, just so you know. And I'm recording this." She wanted to kiss Darcy when he spoke in her ear. "And Riordan is spitting mad and currently making his way to the front of the house. I'm pretty sure that he's not going to be as quiet as you were when you climbed up the trellis and into that window to break into that house. I wish I could have seen that. Good going by the way. You'll have to…sorry, I'm nervous for you.

"I found your emails to Viper and to Gunning. Not very smart of you to think that I'd not find out about them. Gunning is currently in custody, by the way. Just after you left him yesterday, we took him. Burkhardt, too, now that we have his wife and children in custody. Viper won't be free for long. I have a team working on that, too." Tony didn't say anything but smiled at her. "Putting the money in Brewer's accounts and moving it around like you did, that was brilliant. Did you know that you leave a marker when you do shit like that? Everyone knows everything nowadays. There are any number of reasons why I think I should just kill you, but I'm not going to. You've really fucked up, and I want to see you go to prison for it."

"I won't go to prison and we both know it. If anything comes of this, which I don't see happening, I'm going to be killed in a nice, quiet way that will never make a ripple of noise about what I've done." She knew he was more than likely right. "That is if you think you can take me in. How about we take this to my office? I've some correspondence to answer while you go on about things you have no knowledge of." She followed him to his office and blinked several times when he turned on the light abruptly. Storm sat when he did, him at his desk, her in the chair across from him.

"Burkhardt confessed to everything…the money he was given, the fact that you've been working with him and Viper for years now." That made him pale. "You see, we had his wife brought out here, and when they were in the air, I found his involvement in this little plan of yours. Holding her and his child hostage wasn't really something that I'm proud of, but it did the trick. You really thought that having him watch my every move was going to work?"

"So you've caught Burkhardt and Gunning at treason. I'm pretty sure that anything that they say about me being involved isn't going to hold water. I'm a decorated officer. A fucking brigadier general, for Christ's sake. Who do you think they're going to believe, me or two men that couldn't handle the warfare and had to be shipped home in disgrace?" Storm said nothing to him. "I've no idea what you're talking about concerning the rest."

"Too late for that, don't you think? I mean, you've already said that you were careful. What is it that you're being careful about?" Darcy laughed and told her what he could see on the files he'd downloaded. He told her about an account that they'd not found. "You're well-funded, aren't you? Twenty million in an offshore account in the Cayman Islands? Oh, and the money you have in the safe in the basement. Along with fake IDs. You should take better care that you don't write this stuff down where someone can get to it. But you know what I really think is shitty and what got you on my radar? The fact that you were willing and ready to blame someone that was in the convoy with me. Brewer was in the car with me...the driver, as a matter of fact. When I told you he took the picture and sent it, you jumped on that. I had no idea who took it, nor did I have a clue where it was taken until you told me. He was not involved at all, was he?"

"You fucking cunt." She smiled at him. "You think you're so smart, don't you? The almighty Storm Browning has it all figured out and is ready to jump in and save the fucking day. I should have had you killed when we found you hanging in that tree all those months ago. And I would have but for the fact that the president had made it his personal business to come and rescue you."

She'd not been told that he was there. To be honest, anyone could have been there when she'd been cut down and she wouldn't have known it. But this made some of what was going on a little less stressful. The president might be pissed at the way she'd done this...there was little doubt about that, actually. But she knew now that he'd not been involved. That had been her biggest worry.

"Um, Stormy, you might want to back off a bit. There are others listening in on you and Blackson. And since I know you can't answer me, I'm going to tell you. The Feds. They're currently trying to get into the computer that I'm using to pinpoint me. I'm shutting it down." She wanted to tell Darcy thanks, but Tony reached into his desk drawer.

"I wouldn't if I were you. I will shoot your ass if you fuck with me." She was trying to think. If the Feds were involved, then maybe they had been from the beginning. And if they were then the president was as well. Her head was spinning at the possibilities of what the fuck was going on. When her cell phone vibrated, she ignored it. When it stopped, Riordan touched her mind.

*You're about to get some company, love. And it's not me. Move away from the door if you're close to it.* Storm looked out into the hall where they had been only moments before just as the front of the house exploded inward. She saw Tony shift, his tux shredding just as he hit her with his body. Before she could defend herself, even if she thought she could have, shots were fired and she was hurting. Mother fuck, she thought, am I ever going to be well enough to move?

~~~

Riordan paced the hall up and down twice more before his dad stepped in front of him. He was so close to losing it that he nearly took his dad's head off. But the calm look on his face had Riordan rethinking that. His dad was still his dad, and he had too much respect for him to attack him.

"Son, why don't you and I take a walk?" He started to tell him no, he wasn't leaving her. "And in case you didn't get that, it wasn't a request but a command. Don't make me have to use my awesome dad powers on you. The nurses and the rest of the staff are afraid of you. And if there was some news, you're more than likely not going to get it because of the way you talked to them earlier."

"I told her I was sorry." His dad nodded but said nothing more. "And I really wasn't going to tie her up by her ankles and dangle her from the highest pole I could find. She knew that. I was a little stressed."

"As we all are. What do you think Stormy will say to you when she finds out that you've told the entire staff, loudly I might add, that you're married to her and you'll…what did he say, honey?" His dad turned to his mom, and Riordan flushed hotly when she tisked at him. "Ah yes, you said that when she was better and having your children you'd not trust a one of them with the task of birthing them. I'm sure that should it come to that, these people will be more afraid of her than you. Stormy is not a very quiet person."

He knew that, too. When he'd pulled the dead wolf off her body, she looked up at him with blood on her chest. Then when she slapped him in the face, it took him several seconds to realize that he was in the way of the medics.

"What the fuck is wrong with you? Surely you've seen blood before." She spread her hand over her bleeding wound and showed it to him before he could move back. "Blood does not mean I'm dead. It means I'm hurt and you're not fucking helping me by standing in the way of the people that actually know what they're doing. I'm fine, Riordan. Just shot, but really, I'm just fine."

He'd been moved back then and cuffs were put on his arms. He hadn't been sure why that was done until he saw the president. The man was moving through the crowd barking orders like he knew just what he was doing. When he leaned over Storm, he shook his head.

"You just couldn't let me be the hero, could you?" Storm didn't say anything as her T-shirt was being cut away. Riordan nearly passed out when he saw how badly she'd been shot. "You're going to get excellent care, my dear, and some time off for helping us out. I've also had the Feds release poor Darcy. The man nearly shifted twice when they thought he was involved in this. I assured them he was a part of my team. As soon as you tell Riordan that you're going to be fine again and make him believe it, I'll have them release him. I know that he can't shift with cuffs on."

In ten minutes he had been released. Storm was being loaded into the ambulance when he was taken to the office where the president was. After he was briefed, a limo took him to the hospital where Storm was already in surgery.

The walk outside did him a world of good. The sun had long since come up and the gentle rain felt good on his face. His dad said nothing as they walked. Riordan reached into his jacket pocket and pulled out the small black box that he'd picked up yesterday before all this went down. He wanted her to marry him today, but it was a little too hard when she was still in surgery.

"I don't know if she'll say yes, but I'm going to ask her as soon as she's awake. I got her this." The ring box was opened by his dad, who whistled. "I don't think she's a diamond kind of woman. It was pointed out to me once that she's not a chocolate lover either. So I saw this and thought it suited her more than anything. I had to wait on the jeweler to finish the design I had in mind. I think it turned out well."

"It's lovely. And she'll love it. Your mom is going to be jealous of it. Perhaps I can find something for her as well." He told his dad where he'd gone to get it made. "I know that place. Nice place, and locally owned, too. I'll talk to them later."

Riordan looked at the ring. The vintage design was something he'd seen a long time ago. It had been on one of those antique shows where someone had picked the ring up for a song. He'd never forgotten the design and had thought of nothing else since he'd decided to get Storm a ring.

It was a large emerald that was dark with age. Surrounding it on the base were smaller emeralds that sparkled brightly even in the dusky daylight. The tiffany setting was platinum and had emeralds on the posts, too, that were rounded so as not to cut into her fingers when she wore it. But it was the matching band that he loved most. The jeweler had told him that he'd made it for someone long ago and they'd not picked it up. He'd never been able to part with it until now. Riordan showed this to his dad.

The wide band's center was two rows of emeralds that were balanced with diamonds between each stone. Then the entire ring had a row of diamonds both on the top and bottom of the ring that showed well with the engagement ring. He could not wait to see it on her finger and to be able to truly call Storm his wife. His dad handed him back the ring and asked him if he had a date, too.

"I did. But since this is going to take a few days, I've moved it to next week." Dad laughed. "Mom said she'd make sure that the house is ready for a wedding, and the aunts are helping her with all the arrangements. But I was wondering if you'd be my best man."

Dad stopped moving and looked back at him. "You should ask your brothers. This is more suited to them instead of me. It's tradition that it be a younger man, a friend of yours."

"Maybe, but since her aunts are going to give her away, I figured that tradition was out the door. I want you to stand with me when I take a wife. It would mean the world to both of us. Provided that she doesn't kill me before hand." Dad started walking again and Riordan caught up with him just as he started speaking.

"When I asked your mom to marry me, I remember thinking that had my dad been alive, he would have liked Bri more than me. He was forever finding fault with things I did. Your grandmother, my mom, wasn't much better, and I decided that once your mom and I had children, we'd raise them the exact opposite of how I was raised." He looked at Riordan then. "You've done well for yourself and this family. I don't think I've told you this enough, but I'm very proud of you."

"I couldn't have done this without you there to guide me." His dad nodded. "Dad, I'm going to change her when we get home. I'm not waiting until someone else tries to kill her and worry that she won't live. I know that being a tiger doesn't guarantee her living, but she'll stand a better chance if she were hurt."

"Good. And even though she frightens me on so many levels as a human, having her as our tiger will be better." Dad laughed. "I don't suppose you've talked to her about this, have you? I mean, tell her what she'll have to do to be a tiger?"

"She knows. I guess she's done some research on this, with a few of her buddies in the service, and has a better handle on it than I do." Riordan shook his head as they headed back to the entrance of the hospital. "It's going to be an adventure daily having her as my wife. But I wouldn't have it any other way. And our kids are going to be more than a handful. She'll be egging them on, teaching them to curse and to shoot, and no one will fuck with them. I think I'm going to enjoy that, too."

"You're going to make a wonderful father, and Storm is going to be...I was going to say a good mom, too, but she'll be more than that. She'll be the mom that other kids will envy and parents will dislike but respect."

As soon as they were inside, he heard his name being paged. His mom was getting off the elevator just as they were pushing the button to go up. She was smiling, and Riordan felt better already.

"She's out of surgery and doing fine. They're going to keep her under for a little while longer just to make sure that the stitches stay put. I guess they were warned that she can be a bit on the feisty side." Riordan thought that was an understatement. "I thought about contacting you through the link, but I just needed to...."

His mom hugged him to her, and held him while she sobbed out how happy she was that Storm was going to be all right and that she was going to be a part of their family. Riordan held her, thinking how lucky he was that he had such a loving and wonderfully supportive family.

After talking to the surgeon, he was led to Storm's room. The nurse told him it would be a little while before Mrs. Harrison would be brought in, but she'd come with her. Then he was introduced to their bodyguard.

"No one is to go near her unless they are wearing one of these." The man showed him the ID that was hidden under his flak jacket. "If anyone comes to you and asks something, you don't know. If they want something from you, refer them to me. If they...pretty much, if anyone so much as looks at you wrong, tell me. I won't be far from you, but you'll see more than me."

Riordan didn't even ask him if this was necessary. Viper and his men were still out there, and since Blackson was dead, there was no way for them to find out from him what he might know. Riordan sat in the chair and took Storm's hand in his. He kissed the back of it and held it to his cheek as the realization of what was going on hit him.

People were guarding him and his family. They were being escorted to and from everywhere they went until this thing was over. His place of business was being overrun with men in similar dress as the one that was currently standing at attention and letting no one near them. One he'd thought he could trust was dead, and another was currently in federal custody. Storm had taken a bullet for her country, and he was going to be trained in self-defense and handling a gun, as well as being given a long list of things that he could no longer do, thanks to his top secret clearance that the president had gotten for him. And there was a madman out there trying to find Storm.

His future wife was going to find this man and tear him apart, of that he had no doubt. And Riordan was going to stand back and let her. She was better equipped than he was to handle anything the bastard could throw at them. He thought of the conversation that they'd had the morning that Burkhardt's wife had been put on the plane.

"The other phone belongs to Burkhardt. He's in on it with Blackson." He told her that had to be wrong, that he'd been friends of the family forever. "Maybe so, but he's a traitor. Do you remember what I told you about Brewer and that he was with me in the car? Well, Blackson didn't know that and laid blame for this on him when there was no way he could have been involved."

"You've known for a while then that he was in on it." She told him she'd thought so but had not been sure. "And what are you going to do now?"

"Go and find the evidence. It's what I do best." And she had, too, all of it. Blackson had been a traitor to his country almost from the start of his career with the armed forces.

# CHAPTER 12

Viper wasn't a happy man. Not only was the place crawling with armed men, but he could no longer get in touch with Blackson. The man owed him money, and a great deal of it. Even trying his personal number netted him with nothing more than a voicemail request for him to leave a message. And his attempts to reach Burkhardt were getting him nowhere.

Smiling, using his most charming look, he walked up to the woman at the desk who looked like she was close to the edge of screaming. This was the perfect person to talk to when you needed answers. When she looked his way, he nearly backed off. Perhaps she wasn't in the kind of receptive mood he'd been hoping for.

"What is it? If you don't have a number, I can't help you. Take one that's hanging on that wall over there, then have a seat. In case you didn't notice, we're a little on the crowded side." He looked around when she nodded to the packed lobby. It wasn't like there were that many injured people, but the armed men were checking everyone. He looked back at her, and she snapped, "What is it? I'm busy." Viper wanted to kill her right then and there.

"I was wondering about a patient you might have here. I heard that she'd been injured." All he really knew was that the news reporter on the television had said that someone at the Harrison Complex had been hurt and that the woman had been

151

taken here. No other news could be found, no matter how much he'd tried to get it. He had no idea why he assumed it was Browning, but he just knew it was her. "She was brought in from the Harrison building about an hour ago. I heard it on the scanner and was wondering if the family might need me to do something for them." Like he gave a shit if they needed anything. But he was going to find this woman and take care of her, and get the hell out of this country. He despised this place more than he did anything.

"Yeah, let me look it up for you." It wasn't going to give her any more information than he already had, he knew that. He'd already hacked into their system and all he could find was that a female had been brought in and was in surgery. "Says here she's in recovery and that no visitors are allowed in to see her."

That was something new. He asked her if they had said it was Browning. Viper had no idea what her first name was, so he only mumbled past that part when asked. A few more clicks of the keyboard and she looked up at him, frowning.

"Something wrong?" Viper reached into his coat and put his hand on the gun. If there was something there that was going to bring the entire squad of men in the room with him down on his head, he was going out fighting.

"The woman's name that was brought isn't Browning. I can't give you any more than that. But like I said, you can't go and see her. They have her in lockdown." Nodding, Viper left the desk to make his way out of the building. Just as he was near the doors, he slipped into one of the curtained off rooms and waited. He was going to find the bitch and put her out once and for all.

Stepping between the other curtained off rooms, he was careful to avoid the cameras. There was one in each section pointed right at the beds. At the end of the hall, he paused to get his bearings and moved to the hall again. There he found himself right in front of a set of elevators, and standing near the biggest man he'd ever seen.

He was tall, and he had hair that reminded him of a cat. He had no idea where that thought had come from, but it was there, right in front of his mind. A large orange cat that would kill and do so quickly and quietly.

As they both got on the elevator, Viper had a very clear vision of the man ripping his throat out. Again, the image of it was so clear that he put out his hand to stop the doors from closing. There was no way he was riding up with this man. But when someone coming down the hall shouted to a Mr. Harrison, he let the door go and it slid into place before the man coming toward them could enter the opening. When the man turned to him, Viper pulled out his gun and pointed it at his chest. This was going to be much easier than he'd thought.

"Don't fuck with me, Harrison." The man nodded and put his hands up. "When we exit the elevator, you're going to get me to Browning. If anyone shoots even in my general direction, you'll be dead. If I'm stopped, you'll be dead. Anything comes at me—"

"Yeah, I get it, I'll be dead. There is something that you should know, even before we get there. I'm not going to let you touch her. I'll take you to her, even help you get past the guards that are with her, but I'm not going to help you. And believe me, you're going to need all the help you can get when you fuck with her."

"You think so? From what I am to understand, she is incapacitated. And only a woman. She might have others fooled, but not me. I know what she is." He asked him what he thought Browning was. "A whore and a bitch that will pay for the lives that she took from me. Children were on that compound when she had it bombed."

"You do realize that it was you that had those children there. Yeah, I know who you are and what you think you are owed by her. Viper, right? You thought that if the US saw them, they'd never bomb you. So it's you that's to blame for this." Viper hit him with the gun, and the man staggered. He'd not meant to hurt him just yet. He was going to die, there was no doubt about that, but he needed him mobile to get to Browning.

The elevator stopped, and there was no one in the hall. The desk, like the one in the lower level, was there, but it, too, was devoid of people. Even the guard that he'd fully expected to be at a door wasn't there. It was as if the entire floor was not in use.

"Where are we?" The man moved out of the elevator and told him that she was down the hall. "You're lying to me. There is no one here."

"Viper." He heard the woman's voice but not where it had come from. When she stepped into the hall, he wanted to blow her brains out, but knew that he'd need her to get out. The man was no longer any use to him. He started to turn to him and kill him, but Browning spoke again. "You lost, dumbass? You did come here to kill me, didn't you? Well, I have a few things to say to you before you do that. If you don't mind. Oh, you might need to know that Burkhardt has told us all about you."

She was hanging onto the wall. Her gown was thin, and he could see that she was naked beneath it. His cock hardened at the thought of fucking this woman until she was dead, but she laughed at him then. He moved forward, lifting his gun as he went. What did he care if she got answers or not? And Burkhardt only knew as much as he'd let him.

"You shoot me now and how the fuck do you think that you'll get out of here? I'm your only safe way out." He didn't lower his gun but continued toward her. "Blackson sends his love. He's in hell about now, but dead all the same. But before he died—I killed him, by the way—he told me all kinds of things about the two of you. Like how the president was going to be killed in three days. That you have plans in the works to receive a shipment of guns in a week. That's not going to happen, by the way."

Viper paused in mid-step and watched her. She was bluffing. There was no way that she knew that the two of them were together on this. And he'd been told those guns were in port, that all he had to do was pick them up.

"You're coming with me. And if my shipment is delayed, you're going to die in a fashion that will make you suffer in ways that you will never begin to imagine." She laughed at him and lifted her gown up. He'd been wrong about her being nude...her panties were there, but it was the bloodied gauze that had him wondering what had happened.

"Blackson didn't play nicely before he was killed." She moved to the little chair that was just outside the room she'd been standing in front of. "You'll have to wait a bit on me, I'm afraid. Unless you want to carry me. I'm supposed to be on bed rest, but you've fucked that up for me too, haven't you? After you're dead...and you will be...I'm going to go on a long vacation. Not to anywhere that I've been before, but somewhere nice. And quiet. I think I like quiet now."

"Where are your guards? There are any number of them downstairs; why aren't they up here as well? " Harrison was gone as well. Viper asked her where he was, and she laughed at him. "You'll keep a civil tongue in your head, woman, or I'll shoot you now."

"You're very hyped up to have me dead. Let me ask you something while I catch my breath. What did you hope to accomplish by killing me? I mean, you could have done it so many times over the last months. I'm sure that Blackson told you where I was." He said nothing to her. Viper didn't feel he had any reason to explain himself to a woman. Especially this one. "Not talking, huh? That's fine. I think I have it figured out anyway. He dangled me in front of you as the one that killed all your men, when in actuality, he was the one that gave the order. I was just as happy to die hanging there, but he had me doing reconnaissance while I stained your sand red with my blood."

"He said that you had called him on the two way and that you told him there were children on the lot." She was shaking her head. "Why should I believe you when you are nothing but a liar and a woman?"

"Yeah, I'm the last part, no shit, but I won't lie to you. Why do I care if you believe me or not? I'm just telling you what went down. Did you know that he was buying an island?" He felt his heart leap in his chest. It had been his plan as well, to be where no one would ever find him. He could raise his daughter there, make her his sole priority. "I saw the paperwork for it in his desk. You should also know there was a kill order for you, too."

"No." She stood up slowly and moved to the desk. Opening a file he'd not seen, she held it out to him. He didn't move until she laid it on the desk and moved back to the chair. Blood was now seeping onto her gown. He walked to the desk and picked up the file. "This is made up. We were partners, he and I. We did a great deal of work together that netted us both more money than we could spend in two lifetimes."

"Maybe you did, but he was hiding his offshore, and he was getting a lot more than he was telling you, I bet. Was it fifty-fifty, or was it really thirty-seventy, as he was paying you? And I told you, I have no reason to lie to you. What I don't understand is why he was in with you in the first place. Or really, I don't care, but since you think you're going to kill me, I should have answers, don't you think?" He held the gun on her while he read the email. It was just as she'd said, and Blackson was going to kill him. Or have him killed. "He thought for sure that I'd be dead by the time he was going to send this out. My murder, the one that you're supposed to have committed, would have brought some serious heat down on your head. I think it calls me a national treasure at one point. Nice touch, don't you think? He never got to send it, by the way."

"How did you get this?" He looked at her then and noticed that she was very pale. "You are not going to do me much good should you die here."

"Yeah, sorry to fuck up your plans, but you sort of caught me at a bad time." Viper opened the file and saw his name. Not the one he was calling himself now, but his real name. And all the information about him as well. "So, your name is Alhonda Pilchard? I can see why you'd change it. Mine is just what it is."

"I know that your name is Browning. Now that I think on it, Anthony never said what your first name is." She told him. "Storm? As in the weather?"

"Yeah, my understanding is that there was one hell of a storm blowing when I was born. Not sure what the hell my parents were thinking. Did they think that was supposed to be an easy name for me to live with?" She shifted on the seat, and he could see the drips of blood under her. "Why were you partners with him? He never trusted you, I don't think."

Viper looked around. There was no one here but the two of them that he could see. But he wasn't stupid enough to think that she was here alone. Leaning back on the desk, he thought about what was going to happen and why. Laying his gun on the desk, he shook his head as he pulled out his cell phone. One more thing to take care of, and he'd be ready. As soon as he touched the send button, he opened the back of the phone and broke it. It would not stop anyone from finding out what he'd done, but it would slow them enough for the person to move.

"He contacted me about fifteen years ago. There was a shipment coming to him overseas and he didn't want it to get into the wrong hands. He wasn't talking about mine, but the servicemen that needed it. There was a price settled upon, and I took the shipment. I would take about every third or fourth one that came to the men serving." She asked him what had changed. "You did. When you and your band of men began to find my places of hiding, it became apparent that someone was helping you. And so I set him up. When you showed up at the compound, I thought I had him. Then you bombed my home."

"As I have said, it wasn't me that insisted that we take it out. Oh, I'm not saying I didn't help out. I did lead them to you, but it was him that told me that it needed to be taken care of. You didn't bomb my convoy either, did you?" He told her he had not. "Yeah, I didn't think so. But you did take care of the bodies, including Brewer."

"Brewer? I don't think I've ever heard that name mentioned. But I did not care for Blackson for many reasons, as he was lazy and conniving as well. But Blackson owed me money, still owes me a great deal of money, and I kept him around to make sure that I got it. Any way that I could. Burkhardt told us you were in the middle car, and that we were to take care of the bodies and the cars once he or his men had taken care of bombing you. We would do this or we would not get paid. All we were to do was remove the bodies, give the dog tags, which we did not find, to Blackson, and he would take care of the rest." She told him that when they were in country that they rarely, if ever, wore their dog tags, as it was important that the enemy never got that kind of information. "Ah, see, the more I hear from you, the more I think we have both been had."

"No doubt." She moved on the seat again and then sat up. "You do know that you're not leaving here, don't you? I mean, you're not the least bit stupid, so you have to know that this place is surrounded."

"I'm aware that you will try to take me. But I don't think I'll allow that. Prison will not be kind to me." She nodded, and he heard the elevator start to move. "I should like to tell you something before I end this. I have a great deal of respect for you at this moment. You got information from me that I would not have shared with anyone else. But you have helped me as well. There are many things that I'd like to say to you. Killing you, however, is not going to be an option. You were…we have both suffered at the hands of a man that I should have killed long ago."

"She's not going to get very far." Viper felt his heart twist again. "The message was intercepted and someone will find her. I'm to understand you know Mason. He's a vamp that works only for me. Blackson thought that he reported to him, too, but he hated him from the very start. But I've had Mason watching her for some time. I'm sorry, but we can't have her fulfilling your plan. She might run and get out of the country, but your daughter will never get to the home you have for her here. She's not going to make it across our borders."

"My daughter is an innocent in all of this." She sat up then and pointed the gun at him. The bag of blood hit the floor and splattered just as he lifted his hands above his head. "You are very clever. You had me thinking you were close to dying, when all this time you have played me well. I must commend you, Browning. You are as smart as I have been told you were."

"Yeah, I'm a bitch like that. Step away from the gun, Alhonda. And we'll try to not shed anyone's blood today." The doors opened all around them and men with guns pointed at him came from the elevator. He was only going to get one chance at this, and he put his hands down. "Alhonda, don't do it."

"You were a good ally, Storm Browning." Just as he reached for the gun on the desk, his body jerked in pain. So many bullets entered him that he could not think how many had been fired into him. He looked at Browning as he dropped to the floor, and saw her gun was at her side. Nodding as he closed his eyes, he thought her a friend as well.

~~~

Riordan waited until she answered the question, and then he scooped her up into his arms and took her down the hall. If anyone tried to follow them, he had no idea. This was his time. He did hear his dad laughing and wondered if he was keeping them from coming after them. Right now, all Riordan could think about was getting Storm alone.

"You do know that I'm going to have to go back and finish my briefing." He nodded and moved into the room that he'd been in when all this had been going on. "I can't thank you enough for telling me you'd seen him in the ER. It gave us plenty of time to clear the floor of staff and have the men stationed."

"You had the patients moved away already. I did nothing but warn you he was here. Being in the elevator wasn't what I had in mind when I warned you." She asked him what he had planned. "To come up here and ravage you while the others took care of him for you."

"Yeah, it rarely works that way, just so you know." He sat her on the bed and started pulling his shirt off. "What are you doing? I really do need to go back and answer their questions."

"Not now, you're not. Take off that bloody gown please. It's making my cat crazy." Storm nodded and started to unsnap the buttons at the sleeves slowly. "You're going to make him want you. He is already fighting me for a chance to mark you again."

"Let him. And while he's at it, tell him I want him to convert me." Riordan shook his head, but was distracted when her breast was bared for him. "You don't want to change me, or you don't want to do it now? Because I'm sick to death of being at the mercy of other people. Plus, I want to run in the woods like the rest of you do. Your mom said that it's a fucking fantastic feeling."

"My mom would not say fucking anything." Storm giggled as the top of her gown dropped to her waist. "He wants you, Storm. Right now, my cat wants his mate. But we can't change you until we get home. And after the dinner at the White House. I know why we're going."

Her hands stopped cupping her breasts. She was not happy, but Riordan didn't care. He wanted her and she'd have to deal with him knowing why they were going.

"He said it was going to be just the two of us. That the dinner would be in his home and no one would know. Then he invited you guys. And now from what I understand, the families are going to be there as well." Riordan leaned in and took her nipple in his mouth and nibbled on it as she continued. "I don't want this thing. He knows that."

"Lay back for my cat." She did as he asked her to do, and he pulled off his pants. His cock hurt to be deep inside of her, but his cat wanted her, too, and Riordan knew that she loved it when he ate her. "When you come, you'd better be quiet. I think those guys out there would shoot us both if you screamed."

As she picked up the pillow and put it at her breast, Riordan let his cat take him. He was angry with him—his mate was not coming to him fast enough,—but he calmed him with the knowledge that it would be soon. When Storm opened her legs for him and slid her fingers under her panties, he snarled at her. Then he bit into the fabric and tore it from her.

Burying his mouth over her, Riordan heard her screaming into the pillow. Her cream flooded his mouth as his cat lapped at her over and over. When he slid his tongue into her heat, his cat purred.

"More." His cat lifted his head, and they looked at her. "More, purr more. Christ, do you have any idea how amazing that feels? Like being fucked with a huge vibrator that has a movable dick on it."

*Oh, I can do much better. When my cat is finished, I'll show you how much better.* His cat went back to drinking from her, and Riordan thought of all the ways that he was going to make her come. His cat snarled at him, as if to say pay attention to me, when he licked her along her thigh. Riordan never saw it coming, and when he took her thigh into his massive mouth, he couldn't stop him.

His cat took her thigh and bit down hard enough that Riordan heard her bones break. Her scream, muffled by the pillow, had him begging his cat to let her go. When he tore at her thigh, tearing not just flesh but muscle too, Riordan tried to regain control of him when Storm touched his mind.

*It doesn't hurt anymore.* He was terrified that she was going into shock and tried again to get his cat to stop. *No. Don't. He is doing what he needs to do. I can feel his need to make me his. I want to belong to both of you.*

He felt her weaken, but she never stopped talking to him. Sometimes verbally but weakly, other times through their link. She told him of her plans for the house, the color she wanted to paint her office, and what she was going to do to the pool house this summer. Riordan stopped talking to his cat. He was pissed at him, rightly so, but he also knew that he'd never hurt her unless it was to do this. And Storm told him this was what she wanted.

"When we get home, I'm going to have to go into town to get a few things. Will you come with me? And I have to pick up some shoes. I don't have any for this thing." He told her he'd follow her everywhere. "I want you to marry me. If you still want to, I'm okay with it now. I mean, we can do it when this DC trip is over. I have a hankering to be Harrison and no longer Browning."

*I love you, Storm.* She told him she loved him as well. *You should be passed out by now. You're in a great deal of pain, I can feel it.*

"I'm feeling much better. I mean, really good for a change." His cat let her go, and then him. He was standing over her when she looked up at him with the most incredible smile. "I don't think I'm going to pass out at all. And I'm starving."

"That's a good sign." Her eyes drifted closed for a second. Then she opened them again and stared at him, slightly unfocused. "Rest now, love. When you wake up, we'll get married and go shopping for some shoes. I'm excited to see you in a pair of high heels."

Her laughter was soft and faded into a soft snore. Riordan reached for his pants and pulled them on. His shirt, too, as he told his dad what he'd just done. Dad's laughter wasn't as nice or as heartwarming when he told him that his cat had taken the decision out of his hands.

*Perhaps he listens to his mate better than you do. Hasn't she been telling you for days now that she wanted to be a tiger with you? I think it's an excellent place to have this done, too. In the event that there were problems. But as there weren't any, it was fine anyway.* He told Dad that the timing had never been right before, and wasn't really right now. *Well, I'd say that the timing was perfect for him. And I'd not be the least bit surprised if she comes out of this very soon. She was nearly to the point of no return anyway, I think. Perhaps it was the other shifters blood she had in her as well. That girl will never be what you expect, and I'm thinking she's going to give you the time of your life. For the rest of your days. Ours too, if I know her.*

Riordan thought his dad was right. Storm was going to be more than he could have ever hoped for in a mate and wife.

163

# CHAPTER 13

To say she was uncomfortable would have been an understatement. Her body felt strapped down, and she felt naked without her sidearm. Rubbing her foot up over her ankle, she was glad that she'd not mentioned that little piece of metal, and smiled to think that she'd gotten one past the security here. Of course, that feeling was short lived when she thought about what was going to happen within the next half hour.

The man standing next to her wasn't anyone she knew. His name was Ted Branson, and that was about all she knew other than he was Secret Service. He smiled at her twice when she stretched her neck. He was in a suit, but she knew that he was armed to the teeth, and he had a small mike in his ear. She could hear it now, the small buzz of it when someone spoke to him. She wasn't always sure what she was hearing, but Riordan told her that her hearing would calm down after time. She hoped so. Right now she could hear a fly fart in the other room, then sigh in relief when he'd done it.

Riordan had left her when she'd gone to change after arriving at the White House, and he was being seated in the large dining room. Storm glanced over at the table of closed velvet boxes.

"You can look if you wish." Nodding at Ted, Storm made her way to the table. At random, she picked one up.

It was the Medal of Honor. Not touching the actual medal itself, she fingered the ribbon that was folded neatly under it. The men that had died the day she'd been hurt were getting these...or at least their families were. She put it back and noticed that the boxes were labeled, and that was when she realized that Brewer's name was among the others, as it should be. Storm was glad that she'd been able to clear that up for his family.

"I'm guessing that his family knows by now that he wasn't a traitor to his county." When Ted didn't answer her, she turned to him. "I know that he had at least one sister. What happened when she was told?"

"He didn't have anyone. She died some weeks ago. Cancer." Storm stiffened when she heard the president speaking behind her. She turned slowly, trying her best not to muss herself up as she put the box back were she'd gotten it. She'd worked for nearly two hours to get this thing right. He picked up the small velvet box that she'd held in her hands and then put it back to look at her. "Every time I see someone dressed like this, I get all choked up."

"Yeah, well you should have it on. It's just the way that it feels, too." She pulled at the collar, then moved it back into place. "And could you fucking turn the air on? This sucker is wool."

His laughter had her blushing. She was really going to have to learn to hold her tongue. Not soon, but someday. Mom had warned her twice that this was not the place to show what she'd learned in the service. Storm thought that was funny since she'd learned all her language skills in the service.

Her uniform had been in her closet for years. The one and only time she'd had it on in the last ten years was when she'd graduated from the program. But when she'd brought her uniform here, it had been taken from her and pressed, as well as had some additions put on it.

Storm pointed to the stripes on the sleeve and then at the insignia on her shoulders. The president only nodded, and she growled low. With a nod at Ted, the two of them were left alone, and she asked him what this meant. Instead of answering her, he picked up one of the boxes and opened it again.

"Do you know what this is for? I mean, why we honor our men with this? I know you know the definition of what the Medal of Honor is. But do you know why we're giving this to these particular men?"

"They were conspicuously gallant and intrepid at the risk of life above and beyond the call of duty, sir." He told her not to be a smart ass. "Okay, they gave their life that day while in the line of duty. I don't know what else you want me to say."

"They should have had these while they were alive. And would have had I had my way about it." He put the box back on the table and looked at her. "Today, we honor them not for dying on that field that day. Not because their commanding officer ordered their deaths and yours, but because of the mission you were on several weeks before that day. Do you remember it?"

"There were so many." She knew what he was referring to and tried her best not to think about it. "We failed that mission, and you know it. We had a loss of life, and we didn't extract anyone but our own asses. It was a major fail, and everyone from the top of the brass ring to the janitor at the local school knew that it was fucked up."

"Maybe so, but what you did was just what you were told. Even at the risk of telling you that you were right when you told us it was a bad idea, you and your men went in and did what you could. Yes, there were lives lost and you didn't get the man out. But you did eventually, didn't you?" She knew that what she'd done was treason then. And if she had to do it all over again, she'd do the same thing. But her way, not theirs.

"My way was better. It's not always, but this time it was." He nodded. "So you're giving me a promotion and them a medal because I went against your say-so and got the job done. What the hell will others think when they know that you're such a pushover about shit like this?"

"No one but you and I know that it wasn't on my say-so. And you no more believe that I'm a pushover than I think you are. And the others that might have known are no longer with us." He put out his hand. "As for the promotion, I want you to work for me. For the government."

"No." He laughed and took her hand and put it in his. "I don't want to work for you. Every time I do, I get my ass shot to fuck. I'm too old for this shit. I want to retire with grace and dignity. I want to bake and decorate my cookies. Be with my aunts for as long as they have left, if they'll have me. And Riordan and I are getting married."

"Do you even know what those two words—grace and dignity—mean? And as for retirement, you'll be bored within a week. How long can you bake muffins and not want to shoot someone? Not long, I'm betting. But you should know that I'm going to take care of you, as will every president after me, for as long as you live." When she opened her mouth to tell him to fuck off, a man behind them cleared his throat. "Tell them we'll be right there."

"Riordan and I want to have a life, have come children. Soon. We want a family of our own. I want to just...I have a house to fix up." He nodded. "You're not going to let me just go, are you? This is a done deal so far as you're concerned. Well, I'll still be telling you no when I'm nearly ready to step in my grave."

"It is a done deal and has been for a long while. But I'd like to ask you something else, about what you're about to do with me. Your family, other than Riordan, have no idea what this is involving, do they?" She shook her head. "I have a feeling that they think that you're off seeing to something and that when you return to them, you'll be dressed in a lovely dress with high heels."

"You've spoken to Bri...to my new mom, haven't you?" He nodded. "Yeah, I didn't have the heart to tell her that I don't do dresses. She had me pick this sexy thing out, and even bought me some of the toe crunchers. I guess this will really disappoint her, won't it? Actually, I'm thinking I'm going to be a major disappointment to her all the time. She's what my mother would have called dignified and well mannered. All the things I have fought against my entire life. I think that's why I joined up. It suited me to no end that my mother would have been aghast by it."

"Your mother is more than likely rolling over in her grave, even as we speak. And wipe that smile off your face; this is not a good thing. And as far as Bri being disappointed in you, doubtful. I think—and I can't understand why they would—they seem to love you." Storm grinned. "Yes, I thought you felt that way as well. All right then, let's get this started. Are you ready?"

They moved into the next room, and Storm had to pause. She'd met some of the family to the men that had worked for her. Others, most anyway, she had met through their letters and movies that they sent to their sons and daughters.

Storm had tasted Mrs. Winters's fudge from Christmas. It would get to her son about July, but it was still good. Mr. Cartwright had sent his little girl brickle. Storm didn't think that eating it fresh would have tasted any better. But his daughter had loved it and had cried each time the tin came to her. Grandma James had sent her grandson pictures every month…the yard she was working on, the flowers that he'd sent her for her birthday. Storm even remembered the date, January tenth. She'd even shown him how to set it up so that no matter where they were, the flowers would be delivered. When they'd taken some time off to supposedly relax, Mr. Parker and his other son would come to wherever they were and buy them all dinner. Pictures were never taken, of course, but there were some amazing memories. As she moved up behind the president, she looked out over the tables and found Riordan. He smiled at her. Letting out a long breath, she waited for her part in this.

The families were brought up to the podium one at a time. Storm talked with each of them, telling them what she remembered most about their child. How much they had loved them, and how they would talk about them long into the night when they should have been resting.

Two of the parents hugged her tightly, and she wanted to step back. But they needed this, and she was glad in some way that she could help. They had lost a great deal that day, not just in their child's life, but not ever knowing just what had happened the day they were taken from them. When the last family came to the podium, it was the grandmother and with her, she had the daughter of the man she had served with.

"We wanted to tell you thank you." She told her it was her pleasure to have been a part of this. "No, not for this, but for what you did for Alex. He was…they were gonna put him in the prison for his temper if he didn't find some kind of outlet. He'd never lost his temper before then, and he told me it wasn't even his…I don't think he ever got over that until he met you. Alex, he told me that you weren't one to take him whining like a little girl, and you smacked him around a bit."

"I didn't actually hit him, not with my hands at any rate." She smiled and nodded. "Alex was a good man. He just needed to focus on something besides what he thought he should have gotten. And his temper was never a problem when we were working. He'd blow off steam by writing letters to his daughter and using the weights."

"I tried to tell him that, too, but he wouldn't listen to me. Right after he told me that he'd been brought into your team, I did some calling. You'd be surprised what a woman who is determined can find out." Storm knew that was true. Bri was just as nosey. "I had my grandson back because of you. I know that he's gone now, but you gave him back to me at the end. I'll never forget you so long as I live. And neither will my family forget you either. And I got you something."

She started to tell her that she couldn't take it when a tin was shoved into her hands. Storm knew what it was and rubbed the top of the can that had a picture of a huge Santa on it. Storm looked up at her. She had to clear her throat twice before speaking.

"He told me that you collected tins. Said that you'd have a hundred or so before you started cooking for the holidays, and by the end, you'd always need more of them. He sent them back to you. We were always sorry to see it disappear, but thrilled to death to know that you'd be sending him another shipment the next year." She nodded and said that she still had the thank-you notes that they had put in it too. "Alex was brave and a good man. You should be very proud of him."

"I am. And of you. You did something that nobody else could have done. You made my boy into a man. And what a man he was." As she walked away, the president told her to come to him. It was her turn. Turn for what, she had no idea.

~~~

Riordan stood up when her name was called. He moved, picking up things that he'd put out for this on the way toward her. He'd planned this for days now, and he hoped to Christ that she didn't tell him to fuck off. It would be like her to do that, here and now. The podium was moved and flowers were bought out from the back, just as the presidential clergy was stepping forward.

"Dearly beloved, we are gathered here to—"

Storm cut the man off and Riordan closed his eyes when she turned to speak at him. Not to him, but at him. He nearly grinned, but thought for sure that she was armed despite her being checked at the door for guns.

"What do you think you're doing? I thought we agreed that this would be a simple affair and that we'd do this at the court house. At home. In our own town."

"No, you said it would be simple. And this is. Very simple. And we're not having a lot of fanfare, as you said you didn't want. I just chose to have it here, while we're all dressed up and dignified." He looked down at her. "I thought you'd have on a dress, but this is nice. Someday I'll see you in heels, but I guess not on our wedding day."

"You planned this." He nodded, and when she looked at the president, he smiled at her. "You were in on this and you never thought to tell me about it."

"Some things are worth seeing you not know about. We had a slight delay and I had to improvise. That was why I came back to talk to you about the medals. Oh, and you're welcome."

"I'm not thanking you, you jackass." The room erupted in laughter, and she flushed. It was very becoming to see her face bright with embarrassment. "What I mean is, this isn't the way things are done. We should be planning more."

"I planned. You'll do this for me." He leaned to her ear and nipped at it. "I need you right now. And as soon as you say yes, I'm going to take you away and help you get out of this thing before I fuck you."

Her eyes were glazed over with need. Her tiger, nearly always on the edge, moved along her skin and had his doing the same. When she nodded, the clergy started again, and she answered at all the right times. Before he could slip the ring on her finger, she gripped his hand in hers.

"I want to say something." He nodded. "I love you so very much. And your family. More than that, I want to tell you how much I admire you, need you, and how happy I am that you're willing to marry me."

"I love you." She nodded, and he slipped the ring on the rest of the way. Riordan kissed her hungrily and then lifted his head when the clergy told them to face their family. The president came to them and held both their hands as he introduced them as Mr. and Command Sergeant Major Harrison. And that there was a nice reception in the residence for those that wanted to attend. Riordan kissed Storm again and realized then that she'd been called Command Sergeant Major, not just Sergeant Major. Somewhere in the past ten minutes, he knew, she'd been promoted.

As they were congratulated on their marriage, Riordan thought of the things that had happened in the last hour. Notwithstanding, he'd been married to the love of his life, but the things that had come with being married to her had surprised him. Most of it he'd had no idea about. Like her job.

"I told him that I didn't want to work for him." Riordan thought perhaps she'd said that, but he doubted that she really believed it. "I've been promoted, too."

"I can see that." In addition to the smaller star on her stripes, she also had been awarded several ribbons, two of which had not been given out in a very long time. The Medal of Honor was hanging from her neck on a ribbon, and she kept touching it with her fingers whenever she thought no one was looking. The rest he was going to have to have her explain to him, but he was sure she was prouder of the fudge she kept sneaking pieces of than she was all the ribbons and pins on her chest. When Storm moved away from him, his dad came up and put his arm around his shoulders.

"You happy, son?" He told his dad that he had never been so happy. "She's happy, too. I tell you, I've never seen a person take to the conversion like she did. Never in all my life would I have believed that someone would come out of it in less than two hours. But then she's always been on the stubborn side, don't you think?"

He nodded. Riordan thought about how he'd just settled down to wait her out when she sat up on the bed that day. At first he'd thought she was dreaming. He knew that sometimes she had bad dreams that would wake her in the middle of the night. He had reached for her, to help her lay back down, when she smiled.

"When can I shift?" He asked her what she'd said. "When can I be a cat? I can feel her there. She wants out to go on a run."

"You're not supposed to be up yet." He felt stupid for saying that, and she laughed at him. "What I mean is, you should be resting still. Not wanting to go out and play in the trees."

"Why not?" He didn't have an answer for her and told her that. "Then let's go out and play in the trees."

Before he could try to think of a reason that they shouldn't, even if there was a reason out there, he found himself in the empty park behind the hospital in the middle of the night. She turned to him, and he realized how she was dressed and laughed. The sheet that he'd pulled on her when she'd finally fallen asleep was dirty and stained with her blood.

"Yeah, I didn't see anything I had with me that wasn't cut to shit or had blood in it. You think anyone thinks I'm a nut ball?" He kissed her then and pulled the toga wrapped sheet off her luscious body. "I feel like my skin is crawling and my body is hot."

"You're going to run hotter from now on. And you're going to need to eat better. You'll burn more calories as a tiger than as a human." He dropped to his knees in front of her. "And you're going to want to have sex with me all the time, no matter where you are. And so you know, if the urge ever hits you, I'll try my best to make your wishes come true. Or just you coming."

"You mean like I did before, or more so?" He licked the area right over her soft curls. Her soft moan made him slide his fingers into her heat as he watched her face. "You should really get to work there before I bring myself. I told you, my skin is crawling right now."

"Always so impatient. What am I going to do with you?" Her answer had him laughing. "All right, but don't tell me later that you didn't ask for it."

Pulling her pussy to him, he licked her clit until she was riding his mouth. He fucked her with his fingers, her juices running down his hand. When she begged him to stop, he looked up at her and he could see her cat. Before he could tell her to wait, she let her go.

When her cat was standing before him, he thought perhaps he'd never seen a more beautiful sight. And even today, when she'd become his wife, he knew that he would forever remember the way she'd looked that day. She was golden and black, her eyes the color of the emeralds that he'd put on her when he married her. Her cat looked up at him as if she'd known him all along. That she'd been waiting all her life for just that moment when she'd come into their lives.

"Christ, you're beautiful." Her cat moved along his body, marking him with her scent. Riordan ran his hands over her fur, amazed at her softness. "I wish there was more room here so that we could run. But we're in a highly public place, and I don't want either of us to get shot."

*I love your smell. I can almost taste you, it's so strong.* Riordan had let her have her play but kept an eye out for intruders. And when they got home, the two of them ran for miles before they fell asleep in the woods.

"Riordan?" He tried to think where he was when his mom laughed, bringing him back to the present. "Your dad said that you'd zoned out on him and he went to find Storm. He seems to think she's the reason for you not listening to me."

"She is. And I don't mind telling you that she more than likely will be a distraction for a long time." Mom told him that was the way it should be. "I love her. I know that you know that, but I just wanted to tell you that I would die for her. I love her that much."

"Good." They watched her move around the room trying to avoid the president. Both of them laughed when he not only cornered her, but had her picture taken with him by the White House staffer. "She's good for the other boys, too. Darcy is finally getting out of his shell of boredom, and Ennis is thinking of opening his own practice. I know that he has a partnership now, but he was telling me that he wants to be on his own."

"Mac told me he'd have her baby if she'd let him. I guess she's showing him how to be a better people reader. If you had asked me, I thought he was pretty good at it anyway, but he swears he's missing things. I think he's going to be taking a lot of board meetings now with a different attitude. Plus she is helping him swing a deal on a nice house. It's pretty near where we live now, and she thinks she can get if for him for about half the asking price." Mom laughed with him. "Aedan wants to leave the firm. Not that I want him to, but it's time. He's bored, too. I mean, before we left he told me that he thought he could do better behind his own desk. I'm not sure what he meant by that, do you?"

"He's running for the governor's position that is vacant. I think he'll do well at it. He certainly has the right kind of support." They both watched him speaking to the president and the man laughing. Riordan thought that his brother might be in the same position soon if Storm had her way about it. "Liam talk to you yet?"

"No. What is it Storm has him convinced he can do? And she's right, too, all of them are set for bigger and better things, I think." Mom nodded and smiled at him. "Not me. I'm happy with running the family business and having a dozen or so kids, thanks."

"You're happy now because you have her. But when the children come, and they will, you'll want more. If not for you and her, then for them." She leaned against him as she continued. "Liam is going to talk to you soon. And when he does, keep an open mind. If he needs to do this, then you will allow him the freedom to do so."

"What is it I'm agreeing to?" She told him that he'd have to wait for Liam. "But Mom, I don't want to wait."

Her laughter made him smile. Sitting down at one of the many vacant tables now that the awards had been given out and most of the families had gone home, Riordan thought of what he was going to do when he got to go home. He was going to make love to his very beautiful wife.

# CHAPTER 14

"Wait, I don't understand." Storm only nodded. It would come to him sooner or later, and she had time. "What do you mean you've come to arrest me? I've done nothing wrong. I'm just a lousy business man that is losing his shirt."

"Yes, and the millions you have in an account with your fingerprints all over it is going to help take you in for crimes against the state." He looked at the top of his desk, and she sat down on the edge of it. "If you reach for that gun, I'm going to be very pissed at you if I have to kill you. I have dinner plans tonight, and you're not going to fuck them up by making me have to hang around and explain why I had to blow your fucking brains out."

She put her gun on her lap. He stared at it, then at her again. He was thinking hard, she knew it, but right now, she couldn't care less what new lie he was thinking up. Storm kept her eye on him as she thought of all the shit she had to do when she got home. If she got home.

There were people working The Bakery for her and her aunts, who were currently on a much deserved cruise. She had hired seven people to not just cook and run the register for them, but to run the small café that had come from the sandwiches that Bri had introduced to the neighborhood. And business was booming right now.

"I want to make a deal." Nodding, she thought of the deals she had going too. The house for Mac. The building that she and Riordan were buying because it had been too good a deal to pass up, as well as several hundred other things that they had been looking into.

"What do you have to offer me? And when I say me, I mean the government. I'm hoping nothing, but you never know." But she did know and that was what they'd been hoping for. He'd give up his partner in exchange for some of his prison time. It was still going to be a long time, but he might not die in there.

"I have this buddy of mine that I work with sometimes. He has some connections that you might want to know about." This was what she'd been hoping for but said nothing. "I mean, like major connections that will make you kiss me."

"Not fucking likely." When she reached into her pocket for her cell phone, the man nearly screamed. Storm thought it was funny that she had such a reputation that men feared her. She called for someone to come and take his statement. And while she waited she reached for Riordan.

*So, you disappointed you didn't have to kill him after all? I'm not. Dinner is very special. Mac is excited about showing his house off. And I know that you've seen it, but he really is excited.* She told him she was as well. *Hey, I'm glad I have you. Do you know anything about Maycomb Works? Have you had to deal with any of them lately?*

*It doesn't ring a bell, but then I usually don't call them by their names. "Slime ball" and "fucking idiot" are terms I'm more familiar with.* He laughed. *Why do you ask?*

*I had a call from the daughter of one of the owners. She wants to us to come in and revamp the business. I guess they deal in clothing that is made right here in the US. She said that they are losing money because they can make it so much cheaper overseas.* Storm asked him if that was true. *For the most part, yes. But there are more and more people wanting to buy things that were made here. I guess her things are high-end jeans and shirts. Like those kind of things you accused me of wearing not long ago.*

*You still don't have any that are broken in quite right. I guess you need to get out more.* He told her that he was doing just fine. Someone knocked on the door, and she let them in. *I have to go. My transcript guy is here taking the statement. Oh, and I have that thing with your mom tomorrow. She's determined to learn to shoot a gun. Your dad is getting really good at it.*

An hour later, she was leaving the building and headed to her car. Storm had a list of shit to get done today that was three miles long. But she had to do this one more thing or she was going to fall on her fucking face. Literally. She was waiting for Andi Collins to come and get her by the dance studio when she heard someone scream.

"Well fuck me." Pulling her gun and going through the doors to the dance studio, she was careful not to scare anyone else that might be there. When she heard the scream again, Storm took a deep breath and moved to open the door. It slammed back on the hinges before she could even touch it. The man standing there held Andi by the hair while he dragged her along the floor. Storm held the gun in front of her, ready to fire should he fuck with her.

They stared at each other for several seconds before he smiled. It wasn't like she'd never seen this sort of smile before. But this one made her shiver. There was evil there, and a great deal of it.

"Get on out of my way." Storm told him no. "Me and Adrienne have some business to take care of, and you're interrupting us."

"Well, that's too fucking bad. She and I have some work to do to. You see, I need to learn to walk on heels, and I can't do that if you take her out of here against her will." Storm glanced at Andi before speaking again. "Andi, did you want to go with this man?"

"Not so much."

Storm reached for anyone that was close, and she got Ordan. She asked him to come to her.

*I'm on my way. Are we in pursuit of a mad man and you need me as backup? I'm ready.* She told him what she knew. *Ah, a man beating a woman. Not very nice of him. I'm there now. Shall I come back there?*

*No. Call the cops for me. And please get everyone out that you can.* He said that he would do that. She told the man what was going on.

"You can't no way called the cops. You didn't even know what was going on here. Maybe we was having us a round of screaming sex and you done ruined it." Storm had something to say to that, but he continued talking before she could. "I'm gonna leave here now and you ain't gonna stop me. You got no cause to shoot me. I'm an unarmed man."

"He has a gun. He's got it in his hand behind the doorway." That was all she needed to hear, and she fired a shot into his shoulder. As he was falling back, Andi went with him and screamed. Storm entered the room and put her foot on the man's throat.

"Let her go and I won't crush your windpipe. And so you know, you've really pissed me off and I'd like nothing more than to kill you right now. But as I've told one other shit today, I have plans tonight and the paperwork will make me late." Andi screamed again, and Storm knew that he was pulling her hair again. "You really are a fuck wad, aren't you?"

Putting more pressure onto his neck, she watched him struggle to breathe. When he finally let Andi go, she heard Ordan tell her to come with him. Storm held the gun on the man, but didn't let up on his neck.

"I should really end your miserable life, you piece of shit. What the hell did she ever do to you?" Storm laughed when she saw his eyes budge out. "I'll let you talk, but you piss me off more, and I'll simply put a bullet in your empty head."

"My daughter." That was a surprise. Andi looked nothing like the piece of shit laying there. "She's not sending me money when I need it. How the hell am I supposed to live on my pension if she don't pay the bills?"

"Yeah, it really sucks when you have to use your own money to do things like that. What was she thinking?" She pretended to consider it. "Perhaps she figures if you can afford a gun, obviously plenty of food and beer—by the way, you reek of cheap beer—that you're an adult, too, and should be paying your own way."

"Fuck that shit. I have myself needs too. What the hell did I raise her up for if it wasn't to take care of me and mine in my golden years?" Storm thought the man wasn't even close to his golden years, and more than likely wouldn't make it to them as fat as he was. "I'm not going to spend me no time in jail. She'll bail me out or she'll be hurting worse than she is now."

"The police are here and want to come back. All right?" She told Ordan to send them back, that she had him subdued.

It took another hour for the police to get statements and for the ambulance to come and take Andi to the hospital. Her dad, George Collins, was arrested for possession of a handgun without a permit and a list of other shit that Storm just sort of blew off. The handgun possession, and he an ex-con, would hold him for a while. She left with Ordan, and he drove her to her house.

"You want to tell me why you were at a dance studio before you needed me?" She only glared at him. "You're not by chance trying to learn to dance, are you? I'd pay real money to see that."

"How about if I come to the nursing home where you'll be recuperating and show you what I'm learning? Your wife will not be able to take care of you after I finish with you." He laughed, and she smiled. "I'm trying to get the hang of heels. You know, I think I'd rather go to one of those day camps for kids all day than learn this, but Riordan has his heart set on seeing me in a pair."

"So he doesn't know." She told him no. "I won't tell him, but you should ask my Bri. She could help."

"The woman, Andi. I met her a few weeks ago at the bakery. She had a black eye then and some bruises. She was looking for part-time work as the place where she was working, the studio, was going to cut her hours. Didn't know then what was going on other than she was beat to shit, so I asked her if it was possible for her to help me out. She jumped at the chance." He asked her how many days a week did she work at the bakery. "Just three. But she works hard. And, well, with your wife's business doing so well, Aunt Sally asked me to hire someone else."

"You're a very kind person." Storm snorted. Kind person wasn't something that most would call her. "You are. Very sweet and loving, too."

"Now you just went too far." He laughed, and so did she. Storm was trying to be more helpful, but she didn't really care for people all that much. But she had liked Andi. "Her dad said that she paid his bills and he was getting a pension. I wonder what makes a person do that to their kids."

"I don't know, love. I just don't know." As they pulled into the drive of her house, she didn't get out right away. She wanted to talk to Ordan but wasn't sure how to start. "Just tell me. I'm getting used to your bluntness."

"I don't want to do this anymore." He nodded. "I mean, I love working for the president and doing those odd jobs for him, but I don't want to work as a PI anymore. It's…it's fucking depressing. I need something else. The bakery doesn't need me. I hate hanging around the house, and Christ, if I have to go to one more house and serve papers on some jackass that is fucking the neighbor's cat, I'm going to scream."

"What is it you want to do? And I don't even want to think about someone having relations with a cat." She grinned at him. "I see, shock value again? I'm going to have to learn those. But really, Stormy, what is it you want to do?"

"I want to work with Mac." He nodded. "Not Riordan. He'd get less shit done than now, trying to get into my pants all the time. But Mac, he's got it right. Going to businesses and finding out what makes them fail, or not. I think I'd like that."

"I think you'd be very good at it, too." He looked at their home and then back at her. "You're very smart. You don't have to work. You should find you something that makes you happy. And if working with Mac doesn't work out—but I see no reason why it shouldn't—then take the time to find you something that does."

Storm kissed him on the cheek and got out of his car. She felt better now, not just because she was going to work at something else, but that Ordan had told her she was smart. She was, but it was nice to hear someone say it to her. Going into the house, Storm nearly ran up to the bedroom to change. It was going to be a fun night.

~~~

Andi sat on the bed in the emergency room for forty minutes before she decided she was leaving. Her body hurt and the stupid nurse told her she couldn't have anything for it until the doctor saw her. That had been so long ago and no one had come in since, and she was sure they had forgotten about her. Tossing off the sheet, she was ready to stand up when someone came in the curtained off area with her.

"You leaving? And I came all this way just to see you." Andi pulled the sheet up to her chin but didn't lay back down. This had to be a dream. "I'm Doctor Harrison. Ennis if you prefer. The hospital is a little short staffed, and they asked me to come in and help out. Stormy asked me to have a look in on you and I told her I would."

"Storm Harrison, you're her husband?" He said he was her brother-in-law. "Some girls have all the luck."

He laughed, and she felt stupid. Things were forever slipping past her lips that should have been locked behind

183

them. When he asked her to lay back, she did so, but she didn't let go of the sheet.

Andi had been beaten up before. Not just by her dad either. She had a brother and an aunt who took a few swings at her, too. It was why she'd moved out of their home. But fat lot of good it had done her. Now she was not just keeping house for herself, but for all of them. And she was exhausted.

"Stormy said that he pulled on your hair and that this man had hit you a few times. I'm going to examine your head. Then I'd like for you to let me see what it is you're hiding under the sheet." Andi felt her face heat up. "I'm not going to hurt you, Andi. I promise. I just want to make sure that you get the best of care. Stormy will kick my ass if I don't see to it."

"She's very nice. Rough around the edges, but very nice." He laughed, and she felt stupid again. "I'm sorry. I sometimes forget that no one cares what my opinion is."

He lifted her chin up so that she was looking at him. "Why on earth would you think that? And Stormy is rough around the edges; she can cuss badly enough that a sailor would blush. I'm pretty sure that while she was in the service, she might have given lessons to them. And as for your opinion, I'm glad to hear it."

"Thank you." As he examined her, he asked her questions. Some she felt embarrassed to answer, others she did without thinking again. When he was finished, he asked the nurse to set up a room for her. She told him she couldn't afford it.

"Stormy said that she'd take care of it." Andi shook her head. "I'd not argue with her if I were you. She does carry a gun. But seriously, I need to make sure that your concussion isn't that bad. I like to err on the side of caution. Anyway, Stormy said she'd be in to see you later. If not, then in the morning."

"My father. He might—" He patted her hand. "He'll come here if I'm not where he thinks I should be. You must have heard what happened."

"I did, and he's in jail. He was carrying a weapon and there are laws about that." She told him how Storm had shot him. "Good. She must have been having one of her better days if she didn't kill him. She's a shoot-now-and-ask-questions-later sort of person."

His laughter made her smile. And what a smile he had. Andi wanted to run her hands through his thick hair and see if it was as soft as it looked. But she wouldn't. Not ever.

As she lay in her own room with the television bigger than two of her own and soft sheets, she thought of the woman. Storm Harrison was really a nice person. She really was sort of blunt, but Andi liked it. When she was alone in her own little apartment, she would say some of the things that Storm would say. And she would giggle herself sick over how stupid it sounded coming out of her mouth. When the phone rang she nearly didn't answer it, and might not have if the nurse that had brought her a tray of food hadn't told her it was for her.

"It's Storm. I just wanted to see if you needed anything." She told her that she didn't. "My husband and I will be coming by later. I have some things for you. Shit like toothpaste and things. I don't suppose you have those on you."

"No, but they gave me some here." Andi glanced over at the little bag of things she'd been given. "They're very small, aren't they?"

"You should have to share them with a big hulking man." Andi blushed again, thinking of the nice doctor. "Anyway, your dad will be spending a few days in county. I don't think it's going to make him in any better of a mood, but he's not going to come there. Also, I know that you have a brother and aunt at that house. They've been informed and so you know, they won't be allowed in to see you. Nice family you have there. Someone should be taking care of you, not you them."

"My dad thinks I owe him." She felt the tears fill her eyes. "I don't want to have to go back there, but if things don't turn around, I'm going to have to."

"You're not going back. I have something worked out for you when you're released. But for now, I want you to rest and take care. Riordan and I will be by later to talk to you. All right?"

"Yes, ma'am. And thank you." Storm told her it was fine and hung up. Andi lay there thinking of how nice it was to have someone caring for her for a change, then opened the covers on her food tray. "Holy crap. I'm in heaven."

She saw a container of soup with several crackers. A glass of water, three small containers of juice, fruit in a bowl, as well as hot water with instant coffee and two tea bags. There were thick slices of turkey over mashed potatoes, gravy, green beans, as well as some stuffing. In a sealed bag was two slices of bread. On another plate was a slice of apple pie, as well as a slice of cherry, both covered in whipped cream. She found the note when she pulled the napkin off the tray.

*Stormy said to make sure you have a big meal. I had no idea what to order, so I told them to give you the best. I'll see you in the morning, Andi. Your friend, Ennis.*

Andi ate nearly all of it and lay there afterwards and wondered what the heck was wrong with her. It was the most she'd eaten in days, and it had just been too good to turn away. When the nurse came in to ask her if she needed anything, Andi nearly told her that she was fine. But she wasn't.

"Do you think it's possible that I could have something for my head? It's really hurting." The nurse told her that Dr. Harrison had left orders for her to have something and said she'd be back. In less than five minutes, she was back with two little pills and a glass of water.

"This will make you slightly drowsy. But I'll be in to check on you several times, all right?" Andi nodded, taking the medicine and laying back. "Just ring if you need to get up. You'll be dizzy as well."

Andi turned off the light after she left her with the promise that she'd call. But when the drugs started to make her feel really...really light headed, she felt herself drifting off. Andi thought this was going to be the best sleep she'd ever had.

## Before You Go...

# HELP AN AUTHOR

## *write a review*

# THANK YOU!

Share your voice and help guide other readers to these wonderful books. Even if it's only a line or two your reviews help readers discover the author's books so they can continue creating stories that you'll love. Login to your favorite retailer and leave a review. Thank you.

AWARD WINNING, BESTSELLING AUTHOR

Kathi Barton, author of the bestselling series Force of Nature, lives in Nashport, Ohio with her husband Paul. In addition to writing full time Kathi likes to spend time with her eight grandkids, three children and three children-in-laws. She writes to relax and have fun.

Her muse, a cross between Jimmy Stewart and Hugh Jackman brings them to life for her readers in a way that has them coming back time and again for more. Her favorite genre is paranormal romance with a great deal of spice. You can visit Kathi on line and drop her an email if you'd like. She loves hearing from her fans. aaronskiss@gmail.com.

Follow Kathi on her blog: http://kathisbartonauthor.blogspot.com/

www.ingramcontent.com/pod-product-compliance
Lightning Source LLC
Chambersburg PA
CBHW032138170626
46808CB00006B/2288